I Choose You

A Perfect Dish Duo Novel

TAWDRA KANDLE

Cover by Once Upon a Time Covers
Interior Formatting by Champagne Formats

ISBN- 978-1-68230-257-6

Dedication

In memory, with love, of my mother, Jeanne Murray Thompson, and my mother-in-law, Josephine Furfari Kandle.

They were both on my heart as I wrote this story, remembering my own wedding day . . . I am grateful that, for a time even as short as it was, I had these two strong women in my life.

Chapter One

Ava

GOOD MORNING, FABULOUS FOLLOWERS! So glad you stopped by to visit the most happening event planning blog in the cybersphere. And do I have some goodies for you today . . .

For those of you who read Time of Your Life regularly, the Sebastian anniversary shindig went off like a dream. It was a privilege and honor to be part of this couple's celebration of fifty happy years together. We put together a menu that was built around old family recipes and served it on china that Evelyn and Harry had received as a wedding present fifty years ago. Go check out the pictures on our Events page. Seeing their expressions will make you believe in long-term love again.

So what's next? So glad you asked. This weekend, I'll be large and in charge at the wedding of the year. You heard it here first, folks. My good friends Julia and Jesse are finally tying the knot, making it official. Let me tell you a little bit of their love story.

I met Julia during our sophomore year in college, when she began dating my roommate—yes, you remember him, the very popular ladies' man, Liam Bailey. After their—ahem—tumultuous breakup, Julia and her best friend (also her roommate) the lovely Ava, hatched a plan for revenge. I was involved too, but at the time, I didn't realize what the endgame was. I probably would've been caught in the crossfire if Julia hadn't met a certain good-looking guy—with dimples, no less! Hubba, hubba.

Jesse was a grad student in the SLP program at Birch and the son of Dr. Danny Fleming, our favorite science prof. The two met while Jules was working as a part-time nanny for Dr. Fleming's younger son, Desmond. And while sparks flew from the get-go, Julia hadn't abandoned her plot to get back at Liam . . . the implementation of which nearly derailed the budding romance of this weekend's bride and groom.

In the end, our heroine decided true love was more important than getting her own back. All together, now, everyone say, "Awwww . . ."

These two love birds moved in together at the beginning of senior year, and our boy Jesse popped the question the Christmas before Julia's graduation. They had the world's longest engagement, because Julia wanted a June wedding, and Jesse was in the middle of his clinicals last year. But now . . . let the good times roll!

The whole affair is taking place in Julia's hometown. Cliveboro is a sweet little burg nestled in the heart of South Jersey. If I had to choose the setting for a picturesque early summer wedding, this would be it. The ceremony will be held at the bride's home church, St. Philip's Anglican. We're keeping the sanctuary classic and simple, with an abundance of tea roses and babies breath. After the I-do's are exchanged, everyone will decamp to Haverty House, a local landmark and historical home, where we'll first indulge in the chicest of cocktails before the evening gives way to dinner, dancing and dalliance.

Fabulous followers, I'm just crossing my fingers that yours truly can hold back the tears of joy. Because everyone gets a happy ending here. Remember my friend Liam, who played the villain in the Julia/Jesse love story? As it happens, he's knee-deep in the mush with Julia's best friend, Ava. This Italian princess made the man work for her, no doubt, but when I'm around them now, I need flame retardant clothes, because these two are H O T. Will they be the next couple to stroll down the aisle? Both of them are mum on the topic, but I can't imagine Liam's dumb enough to let this precious gem slip through his fingers.

For now, I'm working hard to make sure Julia and Jesse have the wedding day of their dreams. Stay tuned, my friends. Next week every pic you want to see will be splashed all over this site . . .

Until then, stay fabulous. And have the Time of Your Life.

I grinned, shaking my head as I finished reading Giff's blog post. He never failed to amaze me. He'd stumbled into event planning during our last year of college, when he'd put together a few small weddings for friends and acquaintances, but Liam and I were both stunned when he'd announced that he was opening his own business after graduation. He was perfect for the role: he had an eye for detail and some innate knowledge of what would work and what wouldn't when it came to social affairs.

"Ava, we're ready to leave." Julia buzzed into the room, coming to a sudden halt when she spotted me at the desk with my laptop open. "Oh, sorry. Were you Skyping with Liam?"

"No." I turned from the computer, unreasonably annoyed at my friend's tone. If I wanted to video chat with my boyfriend, I was damned well not going to feel guilty about doing it. I hadn't seen him in a week, thanks to all the pre-wedding festivities that apparently required my presence in Julia's hometown. "I was reading Giff's post. He just updated the site about your wedding."

Julia squealed as she came to my side, and I tried not to wince. My friend had never been a squealer until the last six months. I was beginning to think that being a bride brought out the worst in people.

"Let me see!" She bent to look over my shoulder, her lips moving as she scanned the screen. "Oh my God, Giff is such a sweetheart. Wedding of the year. Jesse's mom'll love that." Her voice held more than a touch of resentment.

"Aw, come on, Jules. She hasn't been that bad." I closed the computer as Julia straightened. "I think she's really starting to like you."

"Yeah." She rolled her eyes. "I could tell when she called to remind me for fiftieth time that she doesn't want 'that woman' sitting in the front row at the church. Just how am I supposed to tell Sarah that she can't sit with her husband at his son's wedding?"

"I'm sorry." I rubbed her arm. It was easy to forget how much pressure Julia was under when she was in full bridezilla mode, but I had to admit she'd had her hands full, navigating the delicate balance between Jesse's mother and his father's new family. Since Julia had worked for Danny and Sarah before she even knew Jesse, naturally she was closer to them than she was to his mom, who lived in New York and was uber-sensitive about anything involving her son.

She lifted one shoulder. "Whatever. Jesse said he'd deal with it. He gets pissed when she goes around him to get to me, because she thinks I'll give in."

"And lucky us, we get to go spend two hours with her at the nail salon."

"That's the beauty of having a huge wedding party. There's so many of us that we can make sure she's at one end of the pedicure row while I'm at the other. Plus, Alison promised she'd run interference today."

Jesse's sister had been slow to accept that Julia was in her brother's life for good, but once she had, the two had become good friends. She was a bridesmaid, and according to Jules, Alison was sometimes the only voice of reason between Jesse and their mom.

"It'll be fine. We're all going to make sure nothing happens to upset you before the wedding. That's our job as bridesmaids, right?" I slid my feet into my black flip-flops. "So . . . we're off for mani pedis. Let me grab my handbag from your room." The Coles' house was full to bursting with family in town for the wedding and the bridal party, but I'd somehow scored a prime spot, sleeping in Julia's room. Not camping out in the living room meant I got a little peace and quiet at night. It was probably the only thing keeping me sane.

"You're riding with Courtney. She'll meet you outside. Mom and I are heading over now so we can make sure everything's set up." Julia headed toward the front door as I turned the other way to make a stop in her bedroom. My purse was on top of a pile of clothes and make-up bags in the corner of the room. I dug it out and made a quick stop in front of the full-length mirror on the closet door. My hair was up in a ponytail, with loose tendrils curling around my face. I'd been make-up free all week, mostly because getting mirror time in the bathroom or even here was like fighting the pack for a bite of meat. I pulled my baggy T-shirt tight against stomach, frowning.

I'd always fought the battle of the bulge. It was genetics; I was the short Italian girl with big boobs and ample ass, built just like my mom and both my grandmothers. I'd kept things under control by watching what I ate. When Liam and I started dating, he'd sweet-talked me into trying out running. While I still didn't love it like he did, I appreciated what it did for my body. And okay, I liked the sweaty make-out sessions that almost always followed our runs.

Over the past few months, we'd been so busy with jobs, school and everything leading up to our friends' wedding, I couldn't remember the last time we'd run together. Liam sometimes fit one in between classes, but my schedule was tight. I missed it, and my body did, too, apparently, judging by the extra little jiggle I saw in the mirror. I stuck out my tongue at my reflection and turned off the light as I left the room.

Julia's cousin Courtney was waiting for me in the driveway, leaning against her car. I saw two other girls in the backseat, their mouths moving a mile a minute. Courtney caught my eye and made a face.

"I couldn't take it another second. They're driving me nuts."

Laughing, I walked around to the passenger side. Out of all of Julia's family and friends I'd been in close quarters with this week, Courtney was the one I liked the most. She was older than us, and though she had a wicked sense of humor and dry wit, I could tell her patience was wearing thin.

"At least you get to go home at night. Think of me, being with them round the clock. They never shut up."

Courtney shuddered. "Thank God for small blessings. Let me tell you, my house of chaos, even including the six-month old twins, feels like a day spa after hanging out here. Jules owes us so big."

We both sighed as we climbed into the car. I fought the urge to cover my ears at the sound of Sandra's high-pitched voice. She and Ellen were Julia's best friends from high school, and even though their parents lived here in town, they'd insisted on staying at the Coles' house this week.

"We're bridesmaids! You might need us for something." Ellen stood firm, and Sandra backed her up. "Besides, it'll be fun. Like a week-long sleepover!"

"They're just afraid they'll miss something," Julia had told me when I'd gotten to town last Saturday. "But what can I do? I'm trying to keep the drama to a minimum. Anyway, they aren't that bad."

I had a feeling Courtney would've disagreed with her just now as she backed out of the driveway, her mouth set in a firm line. Ellen finished telling a story that set them both off into peals of laughter, and I hunched lower in my seat.

There was a nanosecond of silence, and then Sandra leaned

forward, putting one hand on my shoulder. "So Ava, Julia says you're in advertising. That must be fun."

Courtney cut her eyes to me, and I bit back laughter at her expression. "Uh, yeah. It's good. You know, it's a job."

"Do you, like, make TV commercials? Or write them? What kind of stuff do you work on?"

"Actually, I handle the social media part of our business. So I deal with putting up posts, maintaining the Facebook pages and Twitter feeds of our clients. I find bloggers who're willing to promote products we represent."

"Oh, so you don't get to meet the cute guys on the ads? You know, like, the models?" Ellen was losing interest.

"No, I don't have anything to do with that process."

Courtney turned the car into a parking lot and pulled into a spot, turning off the engine. "We better get in there before Aunt Heather blows a gasket. We're already running late for our appointments."

I lagged behind just enough to let Ellen and Sandra go in ahead of me, hoping we'd end up in pedicure chairs far apart from each other. But of course, that didn't happen. Instead, the young woman who met us just inside pointed Courtney to an empty manicure station before she directed the other three of us to the last empty massage seats in the row of pedi bowls.

Julia waved to me from the table where a guy was working on her fingers. He grunted something, and she turned back around, shooting me a quick apologetic glance as she spotted her friends sitting next to me.

I climbed into the first seat, which put me between Julia's mom and Sandra. The pedicure whirlpool bath was already filled with water, and I tested the temperature, smiling at the tech to show it was perfect.

Once we were all settled with our feet in tubs of swirling scented water, Sandra turned to me. I guessed our conversation wasn't over after all, since she spoke as though we'd never been interrupted.

"Of course, you don't need to work with hunky models, do you? You're dating Liam Bailey, right?"

Her words carried, high and clear, and I wanted to crawl under my chair. Next to me, Mrs. Cole shifted, and I didn't need to see her face to guess at the expression. To say that she was not Liam's biggest fan would be a gross understatement.

Dating my best friend's ex was a tricky business. I hadn't set out to fall in love with Liam, and I'd fought those feelings for as long as I could. Hurting Julia was the last thing I'd wanted to do. But she'd been long over Liam by the time he and I'd gotten involved. We'd both made our peace with the situation. In the past two years, we'd had moments of awkward, sure, but Julia was so obviously in love with Jesse that I hardly thought about the past anymore.

At least, until the wedding crap had kicked into high gear. At Julia's shower a few months ago, I'd overheard the whispers among her family. Julia laughed it off, but there was no denying that even if she'd moved beyond what'd gone down with Liam, her mother had not. Mrs. Cole got a pinched look on her face any time we mentioned his name. I had the feeling she hadn't wanted to invite him to the wedding at all, but she really couldn't get around it, with me being a bridesmaid. She'd put her foot down at allowing him to sit with me at the head table, though, and I was a little nervous about what would happen tonight at the rehearsal dinner, when they would be in the same room for the first time since Liam had staged his public breakup with her daughter.

I swallowed hard and tried a smile as I answered Sandra. "Yes, Liam and I are a couple."

"That's got to be weird, right? I mean . . . didn't you meet him through Julia? I can't imagine going out with a guy who used to be my friend's boyfriend."

"It was after. A long time after they broke up. And it was . . . complicated." Why was I trying to justify myself to this girl? I kicked myself mentally. "Julia was already with Jesse by the time Liam and I started dating." I glanced across to where Julia's nails were being buffed with such intensity she was gritting her teeth. "And isn't Jesse wonderful? He and Julia are so perfect together."

Sandra sighed. "They *are*. I just want to cry when I see them. The way he looks at her is what I want someday." She shook her head. "But all the good ones are taken, I think."

"Nonsense." Mrs. Cole reached around me to pat Sandra's knee. "You're young. The right one's out there. Look at how many frogs Julia had to kiss before she found her prince."

My face burned. The arch tone of her voice left no doubt that Julia's mom included Liam in the frog category. I bit my lip and schooled my expression to remain as neutral as possible. *Two more days.* I only had to make it through the rehearsal dinner tonight, the wedding tomorrow . . . and I'd be done. I could go home and put this behind me.

My phone buzzed in my handbag, and I slid it out of the pocket. My lips curved into a smile when I saw Liam's name.

Just leaving now. Going directly to the hotel, right?

I tried to keep from squirming as the nail tech used the callous file on my heel. When she paused to rinse off my foot, I took advantage of the break to reply to Liam's text.

Sounds good. Drive safe. I miss you. See you at the church at 6. Do you have the address I emailed you?

He must've been holding the phone, waiting for my answer, because his came swiftly.

Got it, and I will. Miss you too babe. See you tonight.

I put the phone away and lay my head back, closing my eyes as the tech massaged lotion into my feet and calves. Her fingers were magic, and I felt the stress of the week falling away. I missed being touched. Liam gave me amazing foot and back rubs. Of course, his massages usually led to other kinds of touching . . . and I missed that, too. I'd never seen myself as a sensual girl. I'd gone a long time between my first sexual experience, a one-night stand in high school, and the next—which was Liam. But being with him had awakened something deeper inside me, and as it turned out, I liked sex. I loved Liam touching me. And right now, I missed it—and him—with an ache.

Just thinking about it made me want to squirm in a whole new way now. I pulled out my phone again and glanced at the time.

Three more hours until I'd get to see Liam. I couldn't wait.

"NO, DESMOND, YOU NEED to walk slower. Don't sprint down the aisle. This isn't a race." Mrs. Krupp, the church's wedding coordinator, held the blond little boy by the shoulder as she attempted to impress upon him the weight of his duties. Des shook off her hand and pushed out his bottom lip. I choked back a laugh.

I stood at the front of the church, already in position. We'd done the up-the-aisle walk once already, and now they were trying to teach Desmond how to do it. He was the last one to walk before Julia and her father made their appearance.

Scanning the church once again, I frowned. It was six-thirty, and there was no sign of Liam yet. I was beginning to worry.

"Is it just me, or does Desmond look like he might take a swing at this lady?" Courtney leaned over to whisper in my ear. Between us, her six-year old daughter Nala, tomorrow's flower girl, wriggled in impatience.

"I wouldn't blame him. She's annoying as hell." I glanced guiltily up at the altar. "I mean, heck. Sorry."

"At this point, I'm thinking even the big guy's getting ticked off at her."

"Now try it again. Remember, step, together, step, together. And—"

The door at the back of the church banged open, and all

eyes turned to see the latecomer. Liam stopped to ease the door closed, and even from this distance, I could almost feel the tension in his shoulders. In the front pew, Mrs. Cole's mouth tightened.

Julia's voice floated from the side of the vestibule, where I couldn't see her standing with her father, waiting for their cue to practice the aisle walk. "Hey, Liam! You're late. Ave's been worried. Go on in and sit down. We're nearly done."

I smiled, mentally blessing my friend for her grace. It took a special person to be comfortable with having her ex-boyfriend at her wedding, even three years after the fact. Across the altar, Jesse caught my eye and winked. I wondered if he were thinking the same thing about his fiancée. He and Liam had finally come to the point where they were comfortable around each other, and we actually had fun together on our frequent double dates.

Liam came into the sanctuary and slid into the wooden pew farthest back. He scanned the room, and I knew when he'd spotted me. His face relaxed into a grin, and I swore felt the heat of his body all the way in the front. As his eyes scanned me up and down, clearly appreciating my green sundress and the way it clung to my curves, it took every bit of restraint in my possession not to run back and throw myself into his arms.

Instead I focused on the priest, who was motioning to Mrs. Krupp. "Let's get moving, shall we? Send the boy up here. I don't care if he runs, hops or crawls backwards."

Mrs. Krupp sighed in long-suffering patience. Desmond's mother, Sarah, sat near the aisle, and she beckoned to her son. He didn't look happy about it, but he made it to the front with a slow, solemn walk. Jesse held out his hand, smiling, and Des scampered the last few feet, swinging on his brother's arm.

The pianist sounded the opening notes of the Trumpet Voluntary, just enough to start Julia and her dad on their walk. I bit my lip as I watched my friend, clutching her father's elbow with one hand and holding a paper plate covered with the ribbons from her wedding shower gifts in the other. Tomorrow she'd be doing this for real, dressed in the gorgeous cream gown, with the antique lace veil. Tomorrow, I'd be standing up here in front of tons of people, and I'd have to hold it together. Tonight, I could afford to indulge in teary eyes.

As she approached us, Julia glanced my way. She stopped and pointed one pink-tipped finger at me.

"Don't you dare start! None of that."

Behind me, I heard Courtney's breath hitch. Julia shook her head. "You two. Honestly." She plunked her paper bow bouquet into her dad's hand and stepped closer to us, pulling both her cousin and me into a fierce hug. "You know I love you both. But you're crazy. No one cries at the rehearsal. This is when you're supposed to be laughing and making fun of the whole thing."

"It's her fault. She started it." Courtney stabbed a finger into my arm. "But then I looked at you, and I can't believe my baby cousin's getting married . . ." She trailed off into another hiccupped sob.

Julia squeezed us both one more time and then stood back. "Okay, enough now. We need to wrap this up so we can go eat."

The priest sighed and began instructing Jesse, Julia and Mr. Cole on the giving away of the bride. The three mimed the lifting of the veil, the daddy-daughter kiss and the passing of Julia's hand to Jesse. He ran through the entire ceremony, and we all rehearsed filing into the front row to sit down during the homily and Eucharist. Julia and her family were Anglican, close enough to my own Catholic roots to feel familiar, though it still seemed weird to me that their priest was married.

Finally, Julia and Jesse got to the kiss-the-bride part. Jesse pressed his lips to her forehead, and we all giggled: Julia'd told us that they were saving the real kiss for the big day. Father Allan nodded his head, and Julia raised her faux bouquet and let out a whoop.

"All right, people! Time to eat. Anyone who needs directions to the country club, let me know."

Courtney caught my arm. "I take it you don't need a ride to dinner?" She turned her head to look significantly at Liam, who'd stood up and was leaning against the end of the pew. Out of all of Julia's family, Courtney was closest to Julia, and she knew the whole story of the Liam break-up. She didn't hold anything against me, and I was grateful for that.

I grinned at her. "I think I got a better offer. But thanks. Oh . . ." I leaned closer. "And if we don't get there right away, don't send out a search party."

She laughed. "I got you covered, girlfriend. Go get your man."

I managed to maintain a sedate walk across the church, even though I wanted to sprint like Desmond had. I threaded my way around small groups of people chatting, ignoring the tension between the different factions. Sarah and Danny, who stood with Des and Jesse, were trying to pretend Jesse's mom Beth wasn't staring daggers at them. I saw the look of strain on Alison's face as she tried to reason with her mother.

But they all disappeared the second I reached Liam. He slid his arms around my waist and bent to meet my lips as I rose on tip-toe to kiss him. I concentrated on keeping it simple and discreet, trying to remember we were in church. But the minute I felt his body against mine, discretion went out the window, followed closely by focus. All I wanted was more.

I snaked my arms around his neck, trying to pull him even closer. Liam broke his mouth from mine and whispered into my ear. "We should probably take this outside. The priest looks like he's afraid we're going to be struck by lightening, and Mrs. Cole looks like she's hoping it'll happen."

Giggling, I buried my face in his neck. "Let's go. Jules would kill me if I got struck down and messed up the balance in her pictures tomorrow."

He laced his fingers through mine and tugged. I paused just long enough to scoop up my handbag and hook it over my shoulder. Liam held the door for me, and we stepped into the humid warmth of the June evening. He took a deep breath and rolled his shoulders.

"That was hard on you, wasn't it?" I rubbed my hand up and down his arm. "I'm sorry. I could've just met you at the dinner, I guess."

"Yeah, we could've done that, but I didn't want to put off seeing you for any longer than I had to. Sorry I was late. I checked in at the hotel, laid down to channel surf and the next thing I knew, it was six-thirty. Guess I was more tired than I thought."

He unlocked the passenger side door of his BMW, and I got in. Liam's parents had offered to buy him a new car for graduation, but given the tension between them, he didn't feel comfortable accepting it. The BMW was his, free and clear, and it was in good shape. Plus, it held a bunch of good memories for us.

I was ready to make some more tonight.

Liam climbed in next to me, and I reached for his hand again. "You didn't miss anything at the rehearsal except for the glaring war between Jesse's mom and Sarah. Well, to be honest, most of the glaring was coming from Mrs. Fleming. The first Mrs. Fleming, that is. Poor Sarah just looked horribly uncomfortable. Oh, and then there was Courtney and me, holding each other back from strangling the giggle twins."

"The giggle twins?" He raised one eyebrow.

"Don't ask. I have a feeling you'll understand after tonight and tomorrow. Just remember, you've been warned."

Liam started up the car. "Duly noted. Do you have the directions to the country club?"

"I do, but do you really want to go there?" I trailed one teasing finger down his thigh, my lips curving up when I felt the muscles tense. He turned, draping his arm over the back of my seat.

"Don't we kind of have to go? I mean . . . isn't it part of the bridesmaid deal?"

I laid my head against his arm, closing my eyes as I breathed in his one-of-a-kind Liam scent. "Yeah, it is, but I don't have to be there right away. There's an hour of cocktails, people just mingling around. Jesse's mom insisted on it. So as long as we're there by the time they start the toasts, we're fine."

"Hmmm." Liam leaned in to nuzzle his lips on my neck. "So not enough time to make a stop back at the hotel."

"Afraid not. I wish I could, but I'd end up needing to redo my hair and makeup after. We wouldn't make it there on time."

He skimmed his hands up my ribs, his thumbs brushing the sides of my breasts. "I could be careful. Not mess you up."

"Ha!" I moved to give him more access. "Maybe you could, but I can't promise anything. We've been apart for a week. I might just devour you."

Liam growled against my skin. "Oh, babe. You're killing me here."

"I know. Believe me, I feel the same way." I brushed back his hair from his face as headlights from another car illuminated us briefly. "Let's drive over to the rehearsal dinner. Maybe there's a dark corner where we can park. Making out in the church parking lot seems a little tacky to me."

"At this point, I don't care." Liam shot me the smolder, but he turned the key in the ignition and backed out.

I gave him directions to the country club on the edge of town, where Mrs. Fleming was holding the rehearsal dinner. Technically, both of Jesse's parents were the hosts, but I knew from Julia that Danny'd had very little say in the details. His ex-wife was determined to put together an evening that might rival the wedding itself, and it irked Jesse to no end. I told Liam all about it as we drove.

"She's been a piece of work all week. At the bridesmaids' luncheon, she sniped at poor Sarah the whole time. Julia drank almost a whole bottle of wine that night, and from what I heard, Jesse exploded at his mom. I feel bad for him. For both of them, actually. They just want everyone to be happy and get along on their wedding day."

Liam's hands tightened on the wheel. "Yeah, I feel for them, too. It's tough when your parents can't be in the same room with each other without fighting."

I reached over and rubbed his thigh. "I'm sorry. I didn't mean to bring up . . . well, you know." Tracing one finger up to his arm, I ventured a question. "Speaking of that, though, did you call your mom today on your way up here?"

Scowling, he shook his head. "No. I haven't talked to her all week." I felt the tension under my touch and knew with a pang that this time it had nothing to do with being turned on.

"Yeah, I know. She texted me and asked that I remind you it's been over a week since you talked. She's very subtle, that one."

"Shit." Liam's jaw tightened. "Sorry about that. I wish she wouldn't drag you into this mess."

"Hey." I leaned across and brushed my lips over his cheek. "I'm not dragged into anything. If it affects you, it affects me. We're a package deal, right?"

A smile tugged up the corners of his mouth. "Right. I'm sorry the package isn't a little better. More what you deserve, instead of this . . ." He made a rolling gesture. "This fucked up crap. You didn't sign up to deal with my parents' divorce."

I slid my hand down to thread my fingers through his. "I signed up for everything. And from where I sit, the package looks pretty fine." I favored him with a suggestive glance that only made his smile bigger. "Anyway, your mom just wants to hear from you. I don't take sides, but at least she seems to like me, which is more than I can say for the Senator."

"How could she not?" Liam lifted our linked hands and kissed my knuckles. "I know this isn't her fault. My dad's the idiot. But can you blame me for not wanting to listen to my mother go on and on to me about her new life? The guy she's dating from yoga class?" He made a face and shook his head.

"There's a limit to my understanding, and hearing about my mom's sex life is way, way beyond that line."

"Here's the turn." I pointed to the driveway, and Liam slowed, easing the car over the lip of the driveway that led to a large brick house. The sun hadn't quite gone down yet, but tiny white lights already twinkled on the wide porch. We followed the road around to a paved lot, and Liam parked beneath a row of trees, as far from the canopied door as possible.

"Think we're safe from prying eyes here?" He turned off the car and unbuckled his seat belt.

"I hope so. The last thing I need is for Mrs. Cole to catch us making out in the car. She's already not my biggest fan."

Liam sighed and laid his head back, eyes closed. "Sorry. That's on me, too. I'm just a ray of sunshine, aren't I? Maybe I shouldn't have come this weekend."

"No. You absolutely had to come. I wouldn't have made it another night without you. Besides, Julia and Jesse are our friends, and they invited you. They've both moved on. Julia's mom is just . . ." I shrugged. "You know. A mom."

"Yeah." Liam tugged at my hand. "So here we are sitting in my car, secluded from the rest of the world—well, mostly—after being apart for almost a week. Remind me why we're talking about parents? Anyone's parents?"

"I have no idea." I undid my safety belt and shimmied my dress up my legs as I crawled onto his lap, slinging one leg over both of his. Liam gripped my waist, and I lowered myself over him, so that the hardness straining against his zipper met the pulsing need between my legs. He moved his hands under the bunched material to palm my breasts, brushing his fingers over my nipples. I moaned and ground myself against him.

"God, Ava, you feel amazing. Are you sure you can't come back to the hotel with me tonight?"

I bent to match my lips to his, sweeping my tongue in a tantalizing circle around his mouth when he opened to me. Dropping light kisses along his chin, I hummed. "I wish I could. You have no idea how much I wish I could." I spoke against his skin. "But Julia wants all of us at the house for her last night as a single lady. And then we have to get to the hair salon first thing in the morning, and there's the pictures and everything . . ." I sighed, raking my fingers over his hair. "But tomorrow night, as soon as the reception is over, I'll be going back with you. So you better be ready for me."

"I'm ready for you now. More than ready." He lifted his hips up, stroking against me.

"You are." I leaned forward, pushing my breasts into his hands. "Oh, God, Liam . . . couldn't we . . ." I glanced around. No one was parked near us, and it was just about dark now. I could make the silhouettes of people on the porch, but here, beneath the shadows of the trees, I was fairly certain we were hidden. And honestly, at this point, I didn't care if we weren't. Dropping my hand between us, I unbuttoned Liam's pants and pulled down the zipper as far as I could. It was enough that his cock was freed, and I grinned into his eyes as wrapped my fingers around him, making him groan.

"Ava. Oh, God, what're you . . . yeah. Oh, yeah. Babe, that is so good." He was lying as far back in the seat as he could, his hips bucking. "But should we . . . I don't want to make a mess before we have to go inside."

"Don't worry, I already thought of that." I circled the head of his erection with my thumb and kept my tone light, conversational. I knew it drove him crazy when I talked while I touched him, when I narrated what I was doing. "At first, I thought I'd go down on you. Keep it neat that way. But then I was afraid I might mess up my hair. So it just seemed this was a better way to make sure both of us stay presentable enough to make it through this dinner."

I rose up on my knees. Putting one hand between my legs, I moved the thin strip of lace panty out of the way. With the other hand, I positioned the head of his cock at my entrance and sank down.

Liam moaned so loud that a very distracted part of me wondered if they could hear him up on the porch. It didn't matter. I moved over him, riding the waves of pleasure and the feel of him within me.

He untangled his hands from under my dress and yanked down both the neckline and the cup of my bra, exposing one breast and nipple. His mouth closed over the pink tip, sucking it hard until I cried out, holding his head in place. Liam freed the other breast without lifting his head, using his fingers to tease and rub.

"Babe, I'm so close." His lips moved against me, the vibration of his voice making me shiver. "I'm going to come."

"Touch me." I almost growled at him, my head thrown back. "Here—" I caught his hand and thrust it between my legs.

"I know." Liam's fingers fumbled to reach my slick core. "I know. I got you, babe. Come for me now. Come apart around me so I can feel you. Let me feel you."

I cried out his name as every sensation in the world swirled to center at the movement of his hands. Nothing else existed to me but the point where his thumb met my clit and just below where his thick, hard cock slid into me, joining us, connecting us. And then it all exploded, and there was nothing beyond the bursts of light behind my eyes, the sound of Liam's voice, low and hoarse as he said my name over and over, like a litany. He arched up one more time, pumping into me as my body clenched around him.

When I fell down against his body, Liam wrapped his arms around me, pulling me as tight as he could, as much of our skin touching as we could manage. Both of us were breathing hard, our exhales mingling as he kissed every part of me within reach of his lips.

"Do you know how much I love you?" He caught my ear lobe between his teeth, worrying it lightly as he murmured into my ear. "I'm a lost cause, Ave. With you gone this week, I was a mess. I just worked, came home and walked around the house.

And every night, I thought about how damned lucky I am that you took a chance on me, and how even more damned lucky I am that you stick around. I don't deserve you, but I don't care. I'm keeping you anyway."

My lips curved into a smile against the rapid pulse in his throat. It was our mantra to each other, something Liam said to me or I said to him at least once week, borne out of our early days together.

"I love you, too, and I'm keeping you right back."

He sighed then, long and heavy into my hair. "I guess we should probably go inside."

I giggled. "I thought you already did."

"Funny." He straightened both my bra and my dress, covering me, and then smoothed the skirt down as I lifted myself off him. Liam hitched his hip up and pulled out a handkerchief. "Here you go. Want me to help you clean up?"

"No, I got it." I pivoted over into the passenger seat and managed to use the hankie as discreetly as possible while Liam zipped up and tucked his shirt back into the waistband of his pants.

"Ready to do this?" I opened my door and smiled back at him.

"Yeah, I guess. I think I know what the martyrs felt like before they went to the flames." He slammed the driver's side door and met me by the back of the car. "Pretty sure Mrs. Cole wouldn't mind seeing me roast."

"She'll be too busy dealing with Jesse's mom to even think about us. And if she says anything to you, just smile and nod. Don't let her get under your skin."

We followed another couple into the country club. Just beyond the foyer, the main room was filled with people standing with drinks and small plates while wait staff circulated trays.

"Look at that. It's utter chaos, and she's serving skewered meatballs. Meatballs. Kill me now."

I turned toward the lowered voice at my shoulder, grinning. "Giff! I'm so glad you're here."

"Well, peaches, that makes one of us." He scooped me into a massive hug. "But look at you. Goooorgeous." He held up my hand over my head, checking me out with narrowed eyes. "But maybe . . ." Giff tugged the side of the dress down. "There you go." He shot Liam a glance, one eyebrow raised. "Do you happen to know anything about why Miss DiMartino's dress was rucked up on one side, beetle?"

Liam grinned. "I'm pleading the Fifth here, buddy. And claiming immunity since I'm in a hostile environment right now. Oh, and we'll pull in extraordinary circumstances, too, since I was forced to be away from my girlfriend for an entire week. How does that work for you?"

"Hey, man, I'm on your side. If I were you, I wouldn't even be here right now. You got guts, my friend." Giff let his eyes wander back toward the other room. "And you might need them tonight."

"Aren't you on duty?" Liam slung his arm around my shoulders, pulling me against him. I slid my hand over his back and laid my head on his chest.

Giff looked pained. "No. I'm here strictly on a guest basis. Jesse's mother didn't want to use me for her shindig, because she wants it to be completely different from the wedding itself. Read: she wants it to be better than the wedding'll be."

"Which, of course, is impossible since tomorrow is going to be the best wedding ever." I squeezed Giff's arm.

"At least the best wedding to date." He glanced from Liam to me. "Until the couple of the decade decides to make it official, and I get to plan their amazing day."

I shifted under Liam's embrace and changed the subject as subtly as I could. "Julia's so grateful for everything you're doing, Giff. She knows it hasn't been easy, dealing with her mom and putting up with Jesse's mother, too. You've got the patience of a saint."

Giff shook his head just a little, and I knew it was because

I'd dodged his last comment. Planning my own wedding was a slightly sensitive topic these days. When Liam and I'd first started dating, he'd talked about our eventual marriage easily. We both had, comfortable with the fact that it was out there in the future, something we'd get to sooner or later. But ever since his parents' marriage had imploded, he'd stopped mentioning it.

Oh, he still talked about the future—our shared future. I didn't have any doubts about his feelings toward me or his commitment to us as a couple. But I had a hunch that the idea of marriage scared him now. For the first twenty-something years of his life, he'd thought his parents had a picture-perfect union. He'd believed it right up until the day he walked in on his father in bed with another woman . . . and found out that it wasn't just a one-time indiscretion. Turned out the Senator's attitude toward marriage was a lot more liberal than his political stance on anything else.

Liam pulled me a little tighter into him now. "Ava's right, buddy. You're rocking this event-planning gig. So you're sure this is what you want? I mean, you were a poli-sci major. Have you thought about politics? Public service?"

Giff straightened his tie. "I choose to think that planning perfect weddings and other parties *is* a public service. Imagine if everyone had to put up with this all the time." He circled one finger in the air.

"It's not that bad." I waved to Courtney, who was helping her daughter with a plate of hors d'oevres.

"Honey, she's serving mini hotdogs in puff pastry. Better known as pigs in blankets. That's what you give ten-year olds at a camp out, not guests at a rehearsal dinner." He sniffed.

"You're getting dangerously close to sounding stuffy, pal." Liam punched his friend in the arm. "Keep it up and you can start catering parties for my dad."

"Thanks, but no thanks. I prefer not to work for the stiff upper crust. I'm sticking to the fun stuff." He was about to say more, but we were interrupted by Mrs. Fleming's high-pitched voice, calling us all to move into the dining room.

"Dang, guess no pigs in blankets for me." Liam winked and took my hand. "Come on, Giff. You've got to be my bodyguard tonight. Make sure no one stabs me in the back or anything."

"Hey, what about me? I'll be with you all night."

"You're distraction. If Mrs. Cole comes at me with verbal barbs, it's your job to parry those."

I rolled my eyes. "Glad to know I'm useful for something."

Liam leaned over to whisper into my ear. "Babe, you're useful for a lot more than that. Just wait until tomorrow night, and I'll remind you."

I shivered, and he laughed as we took our seats and prepared to get through the evening.

THE DINNER ITSELF WAS not as bad as Giff had predicted. Yes, the food was bland, but it was edible, and since we were allowed to choose our own tables, Liam and I were able to eat with Giff as well as Courtney and her husband. Her daughter Nala was at the table with us, too, and she entertained us with stories of her twin brothers and their puppy. Liam laughed at her as she demonstrated how the babies' heads bobbed around before their necks were strong enough to hold them up.

"Do you have any babies?" Nala, a born flirt, tilted her head and batted sweet brown eyes at my boyfriend. I raised an eyebrow and smirked at him, wondering how he was going to deal with this question.

Courtney took pity on Liam and came to his rescue. "Nala, behave. Ava and Liam aren't married." She raised her gaze to me. "Yet."

Nala wasn't going to be discouraged. "Do you *want* to

have babies?"

Liam looked over at me. "Of course. Some day. If they were guaranteed to be as pretty as you." He winked, and by the way her cheeks pinked, I knew he'd made another female conquest.

"Check you out, beetle. Who knew you were so good with the kiddie set?" Giff nudged me. "Are you keeping your eye on him, peaches?"

"Okay, I have to ask." Courtney stirred her coffee. "What's up with the nicknames?"

Giff grinned. "I've called him beetle since we were freshmen in high school. You know, like Beetle Bailey? The cartoon character? And peaches . . . well, just check out Ava's complexion. Peaches and cream. Especially when you embarrass her and she blushes."

I rolled my eyes. "Thanks, Giff."

A clanking sound drew our attention to the front of the room, where the two families sat at a long table with Julia and Jesse in the center. Danny was standing up, looking vaguely uncomfortable as he held a flute of champagne.

"If I could have your attention . . ." He glanced down at Sarah and then across at his ex-wife. "On behalf of Beth . . . and Sarah . . . and our family, I'd like to thank you all for joining us tonight. For being part of Jesse and Julia's wedding." He turned his head to look at his son, and all at once, the stress, tension and discord in the room melted away in the wake of the love in Danny's eyes.

"Most of you know that the last ten years or so haven't been easy on our family. We've had our struggles, our ups and downs. There were some tough times for Alison and Jesse. About five years ago, I went to visit Jesse at school. He was at SUNY at the time, a sophomore, and like many college guys, he'd started to go a little wild." Danny grinned out at the room. "I'm sure no one else in here has any experience with that." Laughter broke out at more than one table.

"I went to see my son that weekend because I was worried about him. So was his mother." His eyes rested briefly on Beth, and for the first time, I saw a softening in her expression. "I wanted to tell him in person that he was going to be a big brother, and he needed to pull it together." He laid a hand on Jesse's shoulder. "I wasn't sure what was going to happen after I left that weekend. Plenty of kids would've been mule-headed enough to keep on partying, to ignore what I'd said. But I'm proud to say that wasn't our boy. Jesse turned things around, and he worked damned hard to be the man we knew he could be."

Julia leaned closer and rested her head on Jesse's other shoulder. He brought his hand up to touch her cheek, but his eyes stayed fastened on his dad.

"So two years ago, when Jesse decided to come live with Sarah, Desmond and me, I was thrilled. We all were. It was going to be a chance for us to be a family again. And it was great, don't get me wrong. But on the very first day he was with us, he met this girl who'd been babysitting for us. I'm pretty sure he fell for the lovely Julia that same day."

Jules closed her eyes, and even from our table I could see her blush.

"If I'm going to be honest, I'm going to have to say that Jesse stole Julia right out from under his brother's nose, since Des was actually the first Fleming male to lay claim on her." There was more laughter, and Julia sat up, reaching over to pull the blond little boy into her lap. "But Sarah and I couldn't have been happier when those two found each other. We'd known what a wonderful girl Julia is for a long time, and I don't think there's a more perfect couple than the two of them."

A chorus of 'awwws' rose up around the room. Danny motioned both Jesse and Julia to stand as he lifted his champagne high. "Please raise your glasses in honor of my son, Jesse, and the woman who's making him the happiest man on earth, our new daughter, Julia. To Julia and Jesse!"

Everyone echoed the toast, and glasses clinked around the room. Liam smiled into my eyes as we sipped our champagne. At the front table, Danny hugged Julia and Jesse, before passing them along to first Beth and then Sarah. To my relief, no bloodshed or even pointed looks ensued. It appeared a truce had been drawn. For now, at least.

There were a few more toasts, from Jesse's best man, who was a friend of his from college, and from some other family members. Finally, Danny reclaimed the microphone.

"We'd like to thank you again for being with us tonight. I'd like to especially thank Jesse's mother, Beth, who put this amazing evening together." He bowed his head in her direction, and Mrs. Fleming's mouth dropped open before she recovered and smiled. "Now it's time to say good-night, and we'll see you all tomorrow at the church."

A cheer sounded as chairs scraped. Liam took my hand, and we meandered out with the rest of the crowd. Giff grabbed his arm as we stepped into the night.

"You staying at the hotel?"

Liam nodded. "Yeah. You need a ride?"

"If you don't mind. I rented a car to drive up and to use this past week, but Jeff's coming up tonight, so I returned it this afternoon. I snagged a ride here with one of Jesse's cousins. I'd rather drive back with you." He tugged on a strand of my hair. "Are you coming with us, peaches?"

I shook my head, grimacing. "I'm heading back to bridal central with the giggle twins. Pray for my soul. Or maybe for theirs, since I might not make it one more night without smothering them."

"And I'm liable to be her partner in crime." Courtney came up behind me. "You coming with me, chick? I just sent the husband and Nala on their way home, and I even managed to pawn off Sandra and Ellen on Alison. We can have an absolutely silent ride home."

"Think anyone would miss us if we just kept driving?" I

sighed. "I'll be there in a minute. I just want to say good night to Liam."

"That translates to lots of steamy kissing and maybe even some groping." Giff spoke in a loud whisper to Courtney. "It's our cue to gaze up at the stars and pretend we don't notice anything." He made a production of steering her to turn so that their backs were facing us.

Liam slid his arms around my waist. "I wish you could come back with me."

"I wish I could, too. Tomorrow night." I laced my fingers together behind his neck and pulled him down for a kiss. "Dream of me tonight. I'll see you tomorrow afternoon at the church."

"Hmm. Good luck getting sleep. Don't let the gigglers drive you to do anything rash. I'd hate to have to come bail you out." He lowered his mouth over mine again, his tongue making me wish all the more desperately that I didn't have to say goodbye.

"All right, you two. It's one more night." Giff dragged me away, planting me next to Courtney. "Off you go." He kissed my cheek and patted my back. "I'll be by the house tomorrow morning to make sure everything's running on schedule. Try to keep Jules calm, okay?"

"Will do." I waved my fingers at Liam and blew him a kiss behind Giff's back as Courtney began pulling me toward her car.

"It was actually a decent rehearsal dinner." She unlocked the car, and we both climbed in. "Seems like Jesse's parents managed to pull it together at the last minute."

"Let's hope it lasts through tomorrow." I yawned as I relaxed into the seat. "I don't get why people can't act like adults, especially when they know their actions hurt people they love. Like their children."

Courtney shrugged. "It's seldom that simple. Jules told me Jesse's parents had a rocky marriage and an even worse divorce. Beth blames Danny for the whole thing. He's moved on, and she hasn't. Alison and Jesse are in the middle. It sucks."

"Yeah." I was quiet for a few minutes, watching the lights as we passed by them. "Are your parents still married?"

"Yep. Thirty-five years and going strong. Like, disgusting strong. They still hold hands at the dinner table sometimes. But you know what? I love it. It's what I want to give my kids, that kind of example." She glanced at me. "How about yours?"

I smiled. "Yeah, my parents are still married. I think they're more likely to kill each other than talk divorce. I mean, we're Italian, you know? They love each other, but they yell, too. Every now and then, I remember how close they really are. They gave my brothers and sister and me a good strong base." I paused, my mind wandering. "Liam's parents are in the middle of an awful divorce though. It's hard on him."

"I heard a little about that." She shot me an apologetic smile. "Sorry. It's been in the news, and since Julia dated Liam, I feel like I know them a little. But it's got to be rough on you."

"On both of us. Liam's relationship with his parents . . ." My voice trailed off. "It's complicated. That's his favorite word to use about it. They had expectations that he's no longer inter-ested in meeting. And instead of trusting him to know what he wants, they act like he dropped out of college to join a garage band and tour. So whenever we see them, it's tense. And now we almost never see his dad, and he won't return his mom's phone calls, so then she calls *me*—" I broke off. "Sorry, I didn't mean to unload on you."

"No, that's okay. I understand. When someone you love is hurting, it spills over onto you." She pulled the car up to the curb in front of the Coles' house. "Do you think you guys'll get married? I mean, someday?"

I lifted my shoulder. "A year ago, I would've said absolute-ly yes. Now . . ." I fiddled with a string hanging from the hem of my dress. "I don't know. I can't blame Liam for being gun-shy about marriage now. His parents act like they hate each other.

It's ugly."

We got out of her car, locking the doors behind us. "Yes, I get that." She followed me up the front walk, both of us dragging our feet to stay outside and away from Sandra and Ellen as long as possible. "But he was so good with Nala. He seems like the kind of guy who'd be an excellent father."

I nodded. More than once, I'd indulged in a fantasy of having Liam's baby . . . of the two of us, raising a family. But it wasn't something I could let myself think about yet. We were both a long way from that stage of life.

"We better get in the house before Jules sends out the national guard." I climbed the porch steps.

Courtney groaned. "It's going to be a long night." Then her eyes lit up, and she grinned at me. "I just remembered I know where Aunt Heather keeps the booze. Come on, girlfriend. I'll hook you up. We're going to need a nice buzz to make it through twelve hours with the giggle twins."

I gave her a mock salute. "Lead the way."

Chapter Two

Ava

"YOU COULDN'T HAVE ASKED for a prettier wedding day."
I leaned forward from the backseat to smile at Julia. Courtney
was driving us, along with Alison, to the church, where we'd
all dress for the wedding. Mr. Cole had dropped off the dresses
and shoes earlier in the day, while all of us girls were at the hair
salon.

The stylist had twisted my thick black hair into a sleek
updo, leaving just a few strands to curl around my face. She'd
wound a string of tiny seed pearls into it, and I couldn't wait to
see how it looked with my gown.

"I really couldn't. It's a perfect day." Julia was glowing.
There was no other way I could describe my friend. No cold
feet for this bride; she'd slept like a baby, once Courtney and
I'd banished Sandra and Ellen from her bedroom. All morning,
she'd been humming and singing, a virtual ray of sunshine. And
speaking of sunshine, we had it in spades today. Overnight, a
mild cold front had rolled in, taking away the humidity of the

past week and leaving a sky so blue it hurt my eyes and air that was just warm enough to be comfortable.

Giff had breezed through this morning, already dressed to the nines in his gray suit and blue tie. He'd confirmed last-minute scheduling changes with Mrs. Cole and supervised the photographer taking the casual at-home pics Julia had wanted.

"I stopped by the florist this morning, and I saw your flowers. Exactly as you wanted them, and they'll be waiting for you in the cooler at the church when you and the girls arrive. And then I ran by the church. It's gorgeous, Jules. Wait'll you see. Take a peek inside before you get dressed, because I know when you're walking down that aisle, you'll only have eyes for your man."

I was anxious to see *my* man that afternoon. I'd texted with Liam during the morning, and I knew he was relaxing at the hotel, catching up on homework. Working at the university and being in grad school kept him busy. We were both excited for him to finish his masters' degree at the end of the summer, since it would allow him to begin teaching full-time in the fall semester.

But for now, all I wanted was to see his face when he got a load of me in my bridesmaid dress. Julia had allowed each of us to choose our own style of gown; only the color, a bright kelly green, was identical. Mine was strapless, with a sweetheart neckline and a short flared skirt that skimmed my knees. I had fun and flirty silver heels that made my short legs actually look good, and a simple strand of pearls to wear around my neck.

Courtney turned the corner onto the street that fronted the church, and we all ooohed when we saw the steps of St. Philip's decorated with acres of tulle and balloons that bobbed in the gentle breeze. Pots of rose bushes accented each corner.

"It's so beautiful." I sniffled, digging in my purse for a tissue. "It looks just like you told us you wanted it, Jules."

"I know." Her voice held a note of awe. "It's like a dream come true. I can't believe it."

"Well, believe it, sweetie. 'Cause here we are, ready to go make you a bride!" Courtney grinned at her cousin as she parked the car in the lot behind the church.

Inside, everything was bedlam. The florist and her assistants were distributing flowers to the groomsmen and the bridal party. The photographer wandered around, waiting to snap some candid shots. Mrs. Krupp was loudly telling us how long until go time. Courtney and I whisked Julia directly to the bridal room to make sure she didn't accidentally run into Jesse before the ceremony.

"But Giff told me to check out the sanctuary first, remember?" She paused at the doorway.

"I'll go make sure the coast is clear, okay? You wait here." I slipped around the corner and into the vestibule. When I swung open the huge wooden doors that led to the sanctuary, Jesse fell out of them, landing almost on top of me, and I shrieked.

"Sorry!" I pressed my hand to my chest. "You scared the crap out of me."

Jesse laughed. "Me, too. I thought it was a judgment from God, and I was being forcibly ejected from the church."

"Not yet." I smiled and stood back to look him over. "Wow, Jess, you look good. So handsome!"

And he did. The black tux fit him well, and his blue eyes were bright with excitement. He grinned down at me.

"Thanks. So, um, how's Julia doing?" I could tell he was trying to tone down his happy, but he couldn't help the widening of his smile, making the famous dimples pop. It made my heart glad to see that he was as excited about today as Jules was.

"She's walking on sunshine. Not a bit of nerves in that girl." I put my hands on my hips. "But you need to clear out, because she wants to see the church before she gets dressed. And you know the drill: no bride/groom meet-up before the big moment."

"I'll go back to my room." He turned and then stopped

and wrapped me in a giant hug. "Thanks, Ava, for being such a good friend to Jules. I know things haven't been always been easy the last few months, but you've been great. I—"

"Ava? Jesse?" Mrs. Cole stood just inside the vestibule, eyebrows raised as she looked at us.

I wasn't doing anything wrong, but still, I stepped back as though guilty. "Hey, Mrs. Cole. Jules wanted to see the church decorated, and I came to scout it out, make sure it was safe." I pointed to Jesse. "And good thing I did, or there would've been an unsanctioned bride and groom run-in."

She frowned. "Jesse, your father was looking for you. Something about Desmond's shoes." She gave her soon-to-be-son-in-law a pointed smile.

"Okay, I better go see what's going on. See you in the church, Ava." He shot me an apologetic wink before making a quick exit.

"I'll just go tell Julia it's safe for her to come out." I began to slip past her.

"Ava, just a minute. I'd like to have a word with you."

My stomach clenched. I'd managed to avoid being alone with Julia's mother over the last week. Now the jig was up.

"Sure." I shifted my weight uneasily. "What's up?"

"When Julia told us what Liam did to her, I'm certain you can understand how we felt. He hurt her. Deeply. They'd been dating for almost a year, and her heart was broken."

I bit my tongue to keep from arguing with her. Julia had never been in love with Liam, not really. Their time together had been fraught with arguments, more downs than ups, and while Liam had definitely made a huge mistake in how he broke up with her—in front of all our friends at the surprise birthday party she'd planned—ending their relationship had been the right thing to do.

Still, this was hardly the time to contest the point with Mrs. Cole. So I kept my mouth shut.

"I know you were a good friend during those hard days. I

appreciate that. But what I don't understand, and can't understand, is how you could even think of dating Liam after what he did to the girl you call your best friend."

I winced. "It wasn't quite like that. And Julia was already dating Jesse when—"

"Be that as it may. It's just not what's done. Of course, I can't undo it. I just wanted to point out that if it were up to me, neither of you would be at this wedding. My daughter has a much greater capacity for forgiveness than I do. I want you to realize that."

Now temper bubbled just beneath my skin. "Mrs. Cole, today is Julia's wedding day, and I'm not going to argue with you. You're right. Jules is amazing. But Liam doesn't deserve to be treated like a criminal. He broke up with her, and he made a mistake in how he did it. But he regrets that, and he and Julia made their peace. Julia's marrying a wonderful man today. Jesse loves her beyond reason. No one is happier for her than me."

Mrs. Cole didn't move for a minute, and then she turned. "You'd better go get Julia if she wants to see the sanctuary before people arrive. It's getting late."

THE CHURCH WAS FULL to bursting. Late afternoon sunlight shone through the stained glass windows onto the gleaming wood of the pews and the altar, and flowers adorned just about every surface. I stood outside the sanctuary with the rest of the bridesmaids, the mothers of the bride and groom and the ushers. The last few guests were seated, and Giff closed the doors.

"Are we all set, ladies and gents?" He scanned the bunch of us. "Is the photographer ready? Because here comes the bride and her dad."

Julia swept in, clinging to her father's arm. Her gown was an ivory column, with the slimmest of lace strap sleeves holding up the bodice. The same delicate lace ran from the scooped neckline down over the skirt and then gave way to soft tulle. Her light brown hair was partially caught up in the back and fell in huge curls over her shoulders, covered by the light mist of her veil.

There was an audible gasp from everyone in the anteroom, and Mrs. Cole began to dab at her eyes. Jamie and Jennifer, Julia's younger sisters and co-maids of honor, stepped forward to fuss with the skirt. The photographer snapped pictures, and Giff snapped his fingers.

"Bridesmaids! Line up here, please, in the order the lovely Mrs. Krupp gave you last night. Mrs. Fleming, you go in first, and Mrs. Cole, you're next."

I smirked. I knew there'd been some territorial wars between Giff and the church's wedding coordinator; it was why Giff hadn't been at the rehearsal last night. She's made it clear that anything having to do with the ceremony or the church was her responsibility. They seemed to have reached some sort of détente today.

I was behind Courtney, the last bridesmaid before the maids of honor. I watched as she made her way up the white runner that covered the church's red carpet. I held my breath, counting the beats in the music.

"Okay, kiddo. You're up." Giff gave me a little push, and I stumbled forward, recovering my feet just as I stepped into the church. I forced myself to look forward, smiling up toward the altar. I didn't dare look left or right; if I saw Liam, I just might give up and jump into his arms.

I finally reached Courtney and turned to face the congregation. Now that I was safely in place, I scanned the rows until I found the familiar blue eyes, warm and steady on me. I let my gaze linger on him until a ripple of 'awwws' ran through the assembly, drawing my attention back to the business at hand.

Pretty little Nala marched down the aisle toward us, her chin set and in full command of the crowd. She glanced left and right, smiling at her subjects. When she reached her mom, Courtney bent to give her a kiss. I gave her a thumbs up.

And then it was Desmond's turn. I wasn't sure what he would do today, but apparently he'd decided to take advantage of the situation. He strutted, holding the small satin pillow that bore the phony rings, and everyone tittered when he stopped to give one of his cousins a high-five as he passed. He grinned at his father and mother and trotted up to stand next to Jesse.

And then the doors closed again, as the organ fell silent. There was a pause during which it felt as though the whole room held its collective breath, and then the trumpet sounded one triumphant trill.

Mrs. Cole stood up, followed quickly by the rest of the guests. Everyone's eyes turned to the doors, which were flung open by two ushers, revealing the bride and her father. I was watching Jesse, waiting for the moment he spotted Julia. I knew when he did, because a wave of shocked awe fell over his face, and his lips dropped open. He blinked rapidly, making it even harder for me to hold back the tears I'd meant to get out of the way last night. His eyes never left her as she walked gladly toward him and took his hand.

The ceremony passed in a blur of words, standing and sitting. All I could see was the joy on Julia's face as Jesse slipped the ring on her finger. The flash of humor as she nearly dropped her flowers when passing them to Jamie. The mix of happy disbelief and banked passion in Jesse's eyes when the priest finally said, "You may now kiss your bride." The exultation as they lifted their joined hands and danced back up the aisle.

And then my groomsman partner was offering me his arm, and we were laughing up the aisle behind them, spilling into the vestibule where there was a mass hysteria of hugging and kissing.

"Yes, yes, congratulations all around! Now, bridal party, I

need you all to move off to the left here, that's right. Ushers, as soon as we're clear, you can open the doors and guide the guests out to the church yard. Make sure everyone gets a bottle of bubbles." Giff pointed to a basket that held over a hundred small white plastic bottles.

I knew Julia and Jesse had opted to forego the traditional receiving line, since they wanted to get to the post-ceremony photos and still have time to enjoy their cocktail party. We all hid out behind closed doors as the guests made their way outside. I slipped my arm around Julia's waist and leaned up to kiss her cheek.

"Congratulations, Mrs. Fleming!"

Her face went pink, and she grinned, grabbing me in a hug. "That's me! Mrs. Fleming. Oh my God, Ave, did you ever think we'd get here?"

A mélange of memories flew through my mind, from the very first day we'd met in our freshman dorm at Birch, both of us tentative and unsure, to our late-night candy runs, movie marathons and long study sessions at our favorite coffee shop, Beans So Good. I remembered the mess of our junior year, with Julia and Liam's break-up, her early days with Jesse . . . my own misery when I realized I had a crush on my best friend's ex. Even during our last year at Birch, when Julia was living with Jesse and I'd moved in with Liam, we'd stuck close, meeting for lunch on campus and having regular girls' nights.

"I always knew we'd make it." I stepped around her to give Jesse a squeeze. "Take care of my girl, Jesse."

"I promise." He tightened his arm around her shoulder, and I blinked back tears again.

Giff clapped his hands and raised his voice. "All right, bridesmaids, groomsmen—where's my flower girl and ring bearer? Fabulous, kiddos, here you go. Everyone head out. Same order as you went into the church. And after the bride and groom make their big exit, all of you go back into the church for pictures. And . . . go."

This was no sedate march down the aisle. We all dashed out into air that was filled with bubbles and cheering people. I made it to the edge of the crowd and turned to watch the others.

"Hey, pretty girl, got a minute for a lonely guy?" Familiar arms snaked around my waist.

"I don't know. Maybe, but my boyfriend probably wouldn't like it." I covered Liam's hands with my own.

"Eh, who cares about him?" Warm lips nuzzled my neck. "He's probably a loser anyway, letting you wander around here by yourself, looking all gorgeous. Easy pickings for any big, bad wolf who might happen by."

I giggled. "I do happen to have a weakness for big, bad wolves." I watched as Nala and Desmond walked carefully down the steps, Des hopping to pop bubbles with the ring pillow as he went and Nala shaking her head at his antics.

"Do you have any idea how freaking sexy you are?" Liam slid his hands lower to span my stomach.

"You like the dress?"

He growled into my ear. "Yeah, a lot. It looks good on you. But I have a feeling I'm going to like it even better when it's on the floor of our hotel room tonight."

I hummed with anticipation. "I think you may be right."

The doors opened one last time, and Jesse ran out, pulling Julia along. She was laughing, her head tossed back, as they darted through the onslaught of bubbles. They stopped at the gray limousine parked at the curb, and the driver opened the door for them.

"Where're they going? I thought you had pictures." Liam snugged me back closer to him as we watched Jesse load his bride into the car.

"We do. It's all a ruse." I turned within his arms, smiling into his eyes. "They're just going to drive around to the back of the church and go in. But it lets everyone see them leave and the photographer can take pictures. As soon as the guests clear out, I have to go back inside."

"Can I wait here with you? I really don't want go to the cocktail party without you."

I hesitated. My encounter with Mrs. Cole before the ceremony was fresh in my mind, but then again . . . I'd always had a rebellious streak. Okay, maybe not so much a streak as just a speck. But still . . .

"Of course you can. Just hang out in the back of the church. Once the photographer's done, I can ride over to the reception with you." I was pretty sure I was supposed to stay with the rest of the wedding party, but what were they going to do at this point, toss me out? Ban me from the reception? Liam didn't know anyone else here except Giff and Jeff. Giff's work would keep him too busy to hang out at the reception, and Jeff was acting as assistant today. I knew he'd soon be heading over to the reception site to keep his eye on preparations there.

"Thanks." Liam stepped back and let his eyes roam up and down me. "You really do look great, babe. You were the prettiest bridesmaid up there."

"Thanks." I kissed his cheek. "But I think you might be a tad biased."

"Bridal party!" Giff stood on the step by the church door, clapping his hands again. "Back inside the sanctuary, please. Time for the posing."

Jeff was sprawled in a pew, and he offered a hand in greeting to Liam as he sat down next to him. I headed back up to the front of the church, avoiding Mrs. Cole's eyes.

Forty-five minutes later, I was pretty sure we'd been photographed in every possible combination of people and stance. The bride with all the bridesmaids, then with each one on her own, then with all the wedding party, then the bride *and* groom with the wedding party, and then the families . . . pictures inside, pictures outside.

When the photographer finally dropped the camera and nodded, Giff seemed as relieved as the rest of us. "We can all head over to Haverty House. Anyone need directions or a ride?"

I managed to stand next to Julia for a moment. "Is it okay if I ride over with Liam?"

She smiled. "Of course, why wouldn't it be?"

When my eyes flickered toward her mom, Jules made a face. "Don't pay any attention to her. Go on over and get ready to have fun." She gave me a quick hug. "We're gonna dance tonight!"

The rest of the bridesmaids heard her and yahooed in agreement. We were all definitely ready to party.

ALMOST ALL OF MY previous wedding experience had been with my family, which meant big Italian affairs. The reception that followed Julia and Jesse's ceremony was a far cry from the raucous parties filled with too much food, Old World-style dancing and lots of free-flowing liquor.

Because Giff had put it together, everything was just about perfect. But as I sat at the head table, nodding at something the groomsman next to me was saying, I had to admit that I missed the loud uncles calling embarrassing greetings across the room and the grandmothers urging even more food on me.

"So you're in advertising?" The groomsman, whose name was Patrick, was one of Liam's old college friends from SUNY.

"Yes, I am. I work for a firm in Haddonfield." At his perplexed expression, I added, "It's a small town in South Jersey. Farther south than here. Not too far from where I went to college."

"Birch, right? Pretty good school." He picked up his wine, and taking a sip, let his eyes wander down to the cleavage displayed above my gown. "You doing anything after tonight? A bunch of us got a suite at the hotel. We thought we'd take the party over there when it's finished here."

I shifted back a little. "Thanks. I'll mention it to my boyfriend, but we've been apart for a week, so I think we'll probably want . . ." I let my voice trail off. "Uh, a little quieter time. But I appreciate the invitation."

"Boyfriend, huh? Serious?" Patrick leaned closer to me.

"Yeah. I think so. We've been living together for almost two years."

He reached over and picked up my left hand. "But no ring on this finger. Which means you're not completely unavailable."

I tugged my fingers away. "Trust me, I'm unavailable. Completely. I—"

"Hey, babe." Liam stood across the table. "I'm heading over to the bar. You need anything?" His eyes flickered to Patrick's hand, still on the table in front of me.

"Thanks, honey. I could use some more Pinot." I held up my empty wine glass. "Patrick, this is Liam, my boyfriend. Liam, Patrick is a friend of Jesse's from college."

Liam put on the face I recognized from any of the political dinners or parties we'd attended with his parents before their marriage had crumbled. It was a smile that didn't go any further than his lips. He extended a hand. "Nice to meet you."

Patrick frowned. "Liam . . . yeah. Good to meet you, too." He hooked a thumb in my direction. "Ava's been entertaining me up here. You're a lucky guy."

Liam's eyes didn't drop from Patrick's face. "You're not telling me anything I don't know." He leaned over, grasped my chin and kissed me, hard. "Be right back with your wine."

The smile on my face probably made me look like a complete goofball, but I couldn't help it. He was so clearly branding me as his . . . and I loved it. It was a total contradiction of my feminist sensibilities, but somehow that didn't matter. If he'd dragged me off my hair, I wouldn't have complained. I liked belonging to Liam.

Beside me, Patrick sighed. "Yeah, okay. I get it. I don't

have a chance."

I grinned. "Sorry, Patrick. I'm sure you're a great guy. But he's the only one for me. Ring or no ring."

After dinner, there were the toasts. Both of Julia's sisters gave beautiful speeches that brought us all to tears. Her dad's heartfelt tribute to his oldest daughter had me choking back sobs. Then there came the dances: the bride and groom, the bride and her father, and the groom and his mother. During the wedding party dance, Patrick held me a little too close until he caught sight of Liam glaring at him.

When the DJ announced that the floor was open to the rest of the guests for dancing, Liam found me right away and pulled me to him.

"I've been waiting all night to be able to hold you." He fit me to him, crushing my breasts into his chest. "It was all I could not to jump up and grab you when that jerk had his hands all over you."

I laughed softly as I clasped my hands behind his neck. "He was harmless. Just wasn't willing to accept my word that I was taken."

"Hmm." Liam bent his head, covering my lips with his. He coaxed my lips open, and his tongue wandered into my mouth, as familiar and thrilling as the very first time he'd kissed me. I abandoned myself to the sensation, arching my back and press-ing myself into him. His body was hard, all planes and muscles. I ran my hands down his back in appreciation.

"You feel so good. You know every girl here's starring daggers at me now. I think they all wondered who the smokin' hot guy sitting here without a date was." I let my hands roam to his ass and squeezed. "Just need to make sure they know you're taken, too."

"I don't have eyes for anyone but you, baby. Never will." He framed my face with his hands, staring down at me. The music changed to another slow song, and Liam smiled as we heard Frank Sinatra began to sing.

"We have to dance to Frank." I brought my hands back up to Liam's neck. "I'm pretty sure Julia added a few of his songs to her wedding play list just for me."

"She looks happy." He looked over my shoulder to where the bride and groom were chatting with friends at a table just off the dance floor. "They both do, actually. It was a nice ceremony."

"I think they're both ecstatic. The family crap, all the mess of planning the wedding . . . it all sort of disappeared today when she walked down the aisle."

"I hope it lasts." Liam's voice held no bitterness, only a trace of weariness. "I hope they feel like this forever." He rubbed my back as we moved in a slow circle to the rhythm of the music. "Have I told you how much I love this dress? From here, I've got a terrific view of your boobs."

I tried not to smile, but I couldn't help it. "Liam, honestly. It's not like you don't get to see them whenever you want."

"That's not true. If it were whenever I wanted, you'd be naked all the time. But there's something about this dress, too. Very sexy." He ran a light touch over the back of my hair, still pinned up. "How long do we have to stay before we can sneak off to the hotel?"

I sighed and lay my head against his chest. "I wish I could say we could leave now, but there's still the cake cutting. I need to stay until it won't matter if I don't. I'm sorry."

"Don't be. As long as you stick close to me, I'll just keep checking out your rack and thinking about what I'm going to do when we're alone."

The music ended, and I walked with Liam to the bar for another glass of wine. I felt a little light-headed; I'd had several glasses with dinner, and Id never been able to hold my liquor without getting tipsy. The more I drank, the more I relaxed. And the more I relaxed, the more uninhibited I was, which was why an hour later, when they announced the tossing of the bridal bouquet, I was sitting on Liam's lap with my hands in his hair as I kissed him.

"Don't you want to go try for the flowers?" Liam traced the lobe of my ear with his fingertip.

"Nah." I shook my head. "It's for the single girls. I'm not single, right? I'm taken." I wriggled just a little, and Liam fixed me with a stern gaze.

"Be good. If you don't sit still, I'm not going to be able to stand up without embarrassing us both."

I giggled. "If we sat back in the shadows, I bet I could unzip your pants and straddle your lap—"

"Ava." Liam's spoke my name on a groan. "Don't talk like that. Just a little longer and we can escape. But God, woman, just wait'll I get you in that bed tonight. I'm going to make you pay for every little wiggle and every tease."

"Is that a promise?"

"It is. Just make sure you don't pass out on me, okay?" He ran his hands up my thighs over the satin of my dress.

"Don't you mean, pass out under you?" I snuggled closer. "Although I guess that wouldn't be as much of a problem. You could just keep going."

"Not as much fun without partner participation. Besides, I like when you're on top of me."

I tilted my head to kiss my favorite of his sensitive spots, just beneath his chin. "Do you like it when my mouth is on you?"

Liam's arms tightened around me. "Baby, you know I do. There's nothing you do to me that I don't like."

"Ava, there you are." Giff picked up the chair next to us, turned it around and straddled the back. "Didn't you hear? Jules is about to toss the flowers. Shouldn't you be front and center, ready to receive?"

"Nope. The giggle twins have been plotting their strategy all week, and Julia has about twenty other cousins who aren't married vying for that bouquet. I'm not putting myself out there to get knocked around and elbowed for some stupid superstition when I've already got enough man right here, thanks." I took Liam's face between my two hands and kissed him soundly.

"Okay, okay." Giff held up his hands. "I was given the mandate to round up all the single ladies. I didn't want to miss anyone."

"You can now say you tried to round me up, and I would not be rounded." I leaned over, tilting precariously, and patted Giff on his cheek. "Are we about done? How much more wedding is left? Because my feet hurt, I'm exhausted, I'm just a leeetle drunk—" I held up my forefinger and thumb about an inch apart. "And between you and me, I'm going crazy, wanting this guy right here."

Giff grinned. "I forgot how much fun drunk Ava is. Yes, darling, things'll be wrapping up soon. As soon as she does the toss, Julia's going to get changed, and then we'll gather to wave them off. Thirty more minutes, tops. Think you can hold out?"

I groaned, and Liam laughed. "Yeah, she'll make it. I might have to carry her out, but we'll be here." He smoothed his hand over my hair. "By the way, dude, this whole night was amazing. You blew it out of the water. I'm impressed."

I was more than a little tipsy, but not so far gone that I didn't notice the pleasure on Giff's face as he blinked back what I suspected were surprised tears. These two men, each so dear to me, had been friends for almost ten years. They'd seen each other through parental issues, girlfriends, boyfriends, love and loss. They were closer than many brothers, and I loved them both.

Giff cuffed Liam on the shoulder as he stood up. "Appreciate it, beetle. Coming from you . . . well, you know what it means. I need to keep things moving so you can get princess peaches out of here and . . . do whatever it is you crazy kids plan to do." He took off across the dance floor where the squealing single ladies were gathered while the DJ played Beyonce.

Across the table, Jeff smiled. "That was very cool of you, dude. You know how much he respects your opinion."

"I only speak the truth." Liam leaned his forehead against my hair. "Look, she's about to do the toss." He shifted me so that I could see, too.

Julia stood on the small riser at the end of the dance floor. She held up the flowers, and her eyes scanned the crowd of eager women. Turning her back, she did the traditional feign, once, twice and then let it fly over their heads.

I watched the pink roses sail in a high perfect arc—Jules used to pitch on the softball team in high school—and land within the arms of an astonished aunt in the very back of the group. A cheer went up, and Julia clapped her hands as the DJ announced that the final set of songs, the last dances of the night, while the bride and groom prepared for their big departure.

"Do you want to dance one more time?" Liam skimmed his lips along the column of my neck.

"I don't think I can stand up. Can we just pretend we're dancing from here?"

"Sure." He kissed the top of my head and hummed along with Michael Bublé as my eyes drifted closed.

It only felt like moments before Liam dragged me to my feet, and Julia and Jesse were both hugging me, thanking us for being part of their day.

Julia kissed my cheek and took my hand. "I'll text you tomorrow."

"Don't you dare. You'll be on your honeymoon, and I do *not* want to hear from you. Not a word. Call me when you two get home, okay?"

"I will. All right." Tears filled her eyes and leaked down her cheeks. "Ava, I love you. Thank you—for everything—for being there for me—"

"Stop crying, you crazy woman." I pulled her tight against me one more time. "I'm not going anywhere, and neither are you. I mean, except Hawaii. Have a wonderful honeymoon. I'll talk to you in ten days. And not before."

And then Jesse was dragging her away. Mr. and Mrs. Cole

and her sisters closed in around both of them, the Flemings joined them, and everyone waved good-bye, kissing and hugging, crying and laughing.

When the doors finally closed behind the happy couple, Liam heaved a sigh. "Okay, babe, that's our cue. Time to get out of here. Think you can walk?"

"I might be able to, but would you think I'm a total wimp if I said I'd rather have you carry me?"

He grinned and caressed my cheek with the back of his fingers. "Nope. I'd say you're pretty damned smart. Think about how much faster we can get back to the hotel if you're already in my arms."

"OUCH! I THINK I stepped on a stone." I grabbed for Liam's arm and hopped on one foot. The hotel parking lot was dark, but I'd insisted I could walk this time. Being carried out of the reception was one thing, but Liam sweeping me through the hotel lobby was quite another.

"Not surprising. You're barefoot." Liam lifted his hand, from which my silver heels dangled.

"The shoes hurt my feet." I brushed off my heel and took another tentative step.

"So you'd rather walk through the lobby without your shoes than have me carry you."

I nodded. "Yes. Some people might not see my feet, but everyone would notice me in your arms. And they'd think I'm drunk. This way, they just think my shoes were too tight."

I heard his soft laugh behind me as I reached the steps to the door. "Babe, you *are* drunk. Hold on." He stepped around to open the door for me and took my hand., leading me through the lobby. "Elevators are over here."

The doors slid open, and we stepped in. I leaned up against Liam as he braced himself in the corner.

"Hi." I hooked my arms around his neck.

Liam smirked as he looked down at me. "Hi, yourself."

"Did I ever tell you that elevators turn me on?"

His eyebrows rose. "No, I think I'd remember that. Damn. Remind me why we don't live in a high rise."

I giggled and rubbed against him. "Want to know another secret?"

"Sure, why not?"

I stretched to whisper in his ear. "Check in your pocket. Your left pants pocket."

Forehead wrinkled, he slid his hand down, his eyes widening just a little as he pulled out the thin scrap of black lace that was my underwear.

"What's this?" He twirled them on his finger.

"Last time I went to the ladies room, I . . . may have left something off."

His eyes darkened. "So . . . if I did this . . ." He slipped his hand between us, tugged at my dress and slid his fingers between my legs. "Nothing in my way."

I dropped my head. "Nothing at all. Oh, God, Liam . . ."

He parted me with one finger and ran it down my seam. "You're so wet. Do you know what that does to me? Knowing how much you want me?"

I nodded. "I can feel you. Hard against me."

"Do you know what I want to do to you? Right here in this elevator?" His whisper tickled against my ear.

I couldn't speak.

"I want to make you come. Now." He stretched out one arm to the control panel and pulled the stop button. The car jerked to a halt and at the same time, he plunged two fingers into me, stroking and curling to hit the spot on my inner walls that made me gasp. His thumb circled my clit, coming close without touching it. His fingers didn't stop moving, and I rode his hand, clutching at his shoulders as my breath came in short, strangled cries.

"Liam—God, please." I tried to move so that his thumb would finally touch me where I needed it most. But her moved with me, keeping away.

"Please what, baby? What do you want?" He picked up the intensity of his fingers inside me. "Tell me."

"Touch me." It was a cry, a plea.

"I am touching you. My fingers are inside you. Can't you feel them?"

I moaned. "Touch my . . . touch me with your thumb. Please. So close."

"Here?" His thumb skimmed just below where I needed him. "Like this?"

"No. Please. And harder."

Finally, finally, he moved to the small bundle of nerves, pressing with the perfect intensity that I craved. My heart raced into a crescendo as pleasure gripped me, spreading out from my center to infuse every inch of my body.

"Give me more, baby." Liam didn't stop moving. He withdrew his fingers and used them on my clit, not giving me even a second to recover before he brought me up and over the edge yet again.

The elevator began to ding, a repetitive, ear-splitting sound protesting the stop of motion. Liam stroked me once more and then moved his hand, smoothing down my dress.

I was boneless, hanging onto him as he reached to disengage the button. When the elevator began to move again, he bent to scoop me into his arms.

"Nobody's going to think anything about me carrying you now that we're upstairs." He stepped out when the doors glided open. "Our room's right here. Can you get the key out of my jacket pocket?"

I ran my hands over his chest until I felt the thin plastic card. Pulling it out, I unlocked the door, and Liam gave it a gentle kick so we could pass through. He lay me down on the bed, and I closed my eyes.

"Don't you dare fall asleep." Liam kissed my forehead, and I slitted my eyes open, watching him undo his tie and take off his shoes. "I have plans for you. And they involve you being wide awake."

He unbuttoned his shirt and tossed it over a chair. I turned to my side and propped my head up on my hand. I knew I was practically falling out of my dress, lying like this, but I noticed Liam didn't seem to mind.

He unfastened his pants and let them drop to the floor. The boxers he wore beneath didn't do much to disguise the bulge between his legs. Suddenly I was wide awake.

"Come here." I crooked my finger at him, smiling.

Liam sat down next to me, cupping my cheek as he gazed down at me. "Look at how beautiful you are." He leaned down and touched my lips softly with his. "I love you, Ava Catarine."

I twined my arms around his neck and pulled him down to me. "I love you, too, Liam Edward. And I'm going to make you feel so good." I rolled us over and sat up, straddling him. He reached up to run his hands down my arms, and I traced the knots of muscles in his shoulders, across to his chest. Just looking at him, the definition of his pecs and abs made me feel as though I might die if I couldn't touch him. I remembered the early days, when we were just friends and being around him had been like hell. For so long I'd denied myself permission to admit that I wanted my hands on that body. Now I could run my fingers over him whenever I wanted, and I didn't take it for granted.

"Let me take down your hair." He slid his fingers beneath. "Damn, those pins are in there tight."

"Yeah, they don't mess around with wedding hair. Hold on." I lifted my hands to the updo and began the process of hunting for pins, which I dropped into Liam's hand. "I think that's it."

He threaded his fingers through the thick black curls. "I love your hair hanging like this."

"It feels good to have it down." I shook it back over my shoulders.

"I bet this dress feels a little uncomfortable, too." Liam nodded, as though in sympathy. "Why don't you let me help you get it off?"

"You're always thinking of me, aren't you?" I held up my hair so he could get to the zipper. When it was released, the front of the dress sagged, and Liam grinned.

"Why, look at this." He pushed the material out of the way and palmed both of my breasts. "I've been imagining holding these gorgeous tits all night. All week. Reality is so much better than my imagination."

I moved to the side and let the dress slide the rest of the way off me. Crawling back over to Liam, I dropped my lips to his chest and gave myself the pleasure of kissing every inch of warm skin I wanted.

"Your hair tickles." Liam's voice was husky, low.

"Want me to stop?" I paused, my mouth hovering over one flat nipple.

"God, no. Never."

"Good." I resumed my meandering, this time sucking the small brown nub into my mouth. Liam clutched my head to his chest, making a soft noise in his throat. I moved to the other side, to suck and lick it, too. He tasted like summer days and musk, and I only wanted to breathe in his scent as long as I could.

I wandered down his stomach, dropping small kisses along each ridge and running my tongue in circles as I sank lower, following the trail of light brown hair. When his erection brushed against the side of my face, I re-positioned myself to sit on his thighs, letting my hair fall in curtain around my face. I took him in both hands, holding the base and then stroking down with the other hand. My thumb circled the head, mimicking his earlier moves on me.

Liam held himself tense, and I saw his Adam's apple bob as he swallowed. I bent slowly, taking his swollen cock into my mouth a little at a time. His hands moved back to my hair, soothing, encouraging as I took him deeper and deeper, reveling in the texture of smooth skin over the hardness.

When he hit the back of my throat, I lifted back up, sucking in my cheeks until my lips circled just the head again. I swirled my tongue around it, kissing down the hot column of soft skin over the throbbing steel. Taking him back fully into my mouth, I stroked up and down with increasing speed.

"Ava—God, Ava. You're incredible. Ahh . . . wait. C'mere." He gently nudged my head back up. "I want to be inside you. I want to look into your eyes when I come."

I slid back up his body, and once my face was level with his, Liam flipped me onto my back and held himself above me. His chest was heaving with short breaths as he stared down at me. There was something new in his eyes, something intense and serious. He smiled at me and then lowered himself slowly to take my mouth.

As much urgency as I'd seen in him a moment before, this kiss was slow, filled with love, promise and so much tenderness that I felt tears well in my eyes. He swept his tongue between my lips and touched mine so lightly, it almost tickled. He pressed in a little bit harder, tracing a line around my lips. Pulling back slightly, he bestowed small caresses on both corners of my mouth, my nose and my chin.

His mouth continued its journey down my throat, pausing to lick at the pulse on the side, and making its way to the center of my chest. He laid his head down between my breasts, and I shivered when I felt his breath against my skin.

"Do you know how much your boobs turn me on? It makes me crazy when I can see them and can't touch. And when I see other guys checking you out, I just want to punch their fucking eyes shut."

"But you're the only one allowed to see them. And touch them. Doesn't that make you feel better?"

"Hmm." Liam cupped one and kissed the sensitive skin underneath. "Yeah, definitely." He took the pink nipple into his mouth and sucked, hard, so that I felt it in a straight shot down between my legs. I arched my back and held his head, running my fingers through his soft brown hair.

"Feels so good." I gasped as he bit softly and then moved to the other side, repeating everything he'd just done. "Liam . . . so good."

He smiled and whispered against me. "Wanna bet I can make it even better?" He slid his hand between my legs again. "Mmmm . . . still wet." Two fingers closed in a pinch around my clit, and I raised my hips, undulating against his hand to find the perfect rhythm. He was relentless, never stopping as pleasure built up once more until I thought I'd die.

As the orgasm gripped my body, Liam pushed up to kneel between my legs and thrust into me. He lifted my hips, adjusting the angle so that his cock hit just the right spot inside me. I gripped the sheets beneath me in clenched hands and tilted back my head.

"No—look here, at me. Right in my eyes, baby. I want you to see how much I love you and feel it right down to your soul, in every inch of your body. Look at me. Look into me."

I fastened my eyes to the steadfast blue of his as I rose to another climax. Love infused all of me, every movement he made, and when at last I cried out his name, my inner channels spasmed around him, and Liam's body tensed into one hard muscle as he came.

He fell next to me onto the bed. The wine, the long day and a body that was replete with satisfaction caught up with me, and I felt myself sliding toward oblivion.

Liam wrapped his arms around my stomach and pulled me back against his chest. He nuzzled my neck, and I hummed in appreciation.

"Don't leave me, okay?" I was only half-awake and still a little drunk, but nevertheless, I knew that falling asleep in his arms after a week apart felt so good. I covered his hands with my own and held on tight.

"Never, baby. I promise. Never."

Chapter Three

Liam

NO MATTER HOW LONG I'd been with Ava, shared her bed, lived in the same house . . . . I never got tired of waking up with her in my arms. I loved watching her sleep, her face relaxed and her hair messed up. Usually I was the one who'd messed it up, so maybe that was part of it, too.

I wasn't ashamed to admit that her being away the week before had been excruciating. We'd been spoiled over the past few years, in that we hadn't had been to be apart more than maybe a night or two. And even that was rare. I had a lot of faults, but being stupid wasn't one of them. Once Ava was really and truly mine, I was smart enough to make sure I held on tight. She was the best thing that ever happened to me, and I wasn't ever going to let her go.

Which brought me back to the small black velvet box that was shoved deep in my duffle bag.

I'd always pictured myself getting married one day, but it hadn't been more than a hazy dream until I'd met Ava. And then it became my goal. I knew we had to wait a little while, because when I'd made the decision to go to grad school right after college, it meant turning my back on the career my parents had laid out for me—and saying good-bye to their financial support, too. My job at the university was great, but it didn't pay enough yet to support us. Ava's salary helped, but Id wanted more for us before we made it official.

And then when my mom found out that my father was cheating on her—and had been for a long, long time—and filed for divorce, I'd made up my mind to wait until things settled down. I still wanted to marry Ava, but getting engaged and planning a wedding while my parents were at each other's throats didn't sound like fun to me. I wanted to spare us all that mess. Not to mention, the local press had picked up the story of my mom and dad's divorce. It was the kind of tabloid shit they loved, and no way was I dragging Ava into that any more than she had to be.

Unfortunately, my parents were both dragging the whole thing out, and it didn't show a sign of ending any time soon. And I'd decided I wasn't waiting anymore.

Ava was mine. It was time to make it official.

I had a plan. It involved a moonlight walk on campus, hitting all the spots that meant something to both us and ending up on the bench just outside the dorm I'd lived in during junior year. That was where I planned to drop to one traditional knee and propose.

I'd already talked to Ava's dad. It hadn't been easy to get Mr. DiMartino by himself; the family was always there, together, everyone talking all at once. Since we visited her family once a month or so, I'd gotten used to it, and I even liked it now. But all that togetherness made private conversation tough. I'd managed to do it finally one Sunday when Ava, her mom and her sister-in-law Angela went out together to do some shopping for baby stuff. Ange was pregnant, and they'd just found out she and Carl were having a boy. Apparently that meant they could plan the nursery now, or so all the women said.

I'd stayed behind at the house with Ava's dad and her brothers, Carl and Vince. There was a Phillies game on TV and a huge platter of antipasto on the coffee table. The family restaurant, Cucina Felice, was closed on Sundays, making it the one day of the week I was likely to find Anthony DiMartino away from his kitchen.

I waited for ten minutes after the women left, just in case they came back for anything. And then I took a deep breath and cleared my throat.

"Mr. DiMartino?"

He glanced my way. "Yeah?"

"Uh, I was wondering if I could talk to you for a minute."

His eyes stayed glued on the screen. "Sure. What's up?"

I swallowed hard. The DiMartinos had taken me into their family without hesitation. I was treated like a son, like a brother, and for that I was grateful. There was more affection and acceptance than I'd ever known from my own blood relations, who were reserved and cool. But still . . . I knew how they all felt about Ava. She was the princess of the family. The only daughter left to them after Antonia had been killed by a drunk driver some years back. They liked me, sure, but I was still nervous as hell.

"Uh, I was wondering . . ." I rubbed my hands over my jeans. Suddenly my palms were sweaty. "Um, could we maybe talk . . . in the other room?"

Now all three men were looking at me. Vince's brows were drawn together, a certain sign that he was getting annoyed—probably because I was interrupting the game—but Carl grinned at me.

"Oh, so that's how it is, huh?" He laughed and reached over to slap me on the back. "'Bout time, man."

Mr. DiMartino stood up. "Sure. Come on in the kitchen." He picked up the nearly-empty platter. "I'll cut some more meats and cheese for us."

57

I followed him across the room, while Carl continued to chuckle and Vince asked, "What's going on? What're you talking about?"

In the kitchen, Ava's dad opened the fridge and began pulling out packages of cold cuts. "So, go ahead. Talk."

I took another breath. I'd practiced this in my head, but doing it for real was harder than I'd thought. Especially with my girlfriend's father standing across from, holding a large knife as he sliced salami. "Um, okay. I hope you and Mrs. DiMartino know how much Ava means to me. And how much it means that your family has been so great to me." I licked my lips. "Ava and I've been together for over two years now, and I'm going to be done with grad school this summer. Birch has already offered me a full-time job in the history department. It won't be a lot of money at first, but it'll be a good start, I think." I stared at a spot on the counter, just beyond Mr. DiMartino. "I'd like to ask Ava to marry me."

Mr. DiMartino had moved on to slicing a block of provolone cheese, and to his credit, he didn't flinch. "Aha. I see. And you're coming to me why?"

I frowned. "I wanted to ask your permission. To . . . to propose to your daughter." The words finally sank into my mind, and I spit them out. "I'd like your blessing to ask Ava to marry me."

Now a broad smile spread across the man's face, and he set down the knife. *That was a good sign, right?*

"Liam, my boy, thank you. Not many young men would have the respect nowadays to ask the father for the daughter's hand. It means something." He reached out and offered me his own hand, which I took. He closed it over mine in a tight grip and shook it.

"Ava Catarine is special, you know. She has it in her head that Antonia, may God rest her soul—" He crossed himself, and I wished I could do the same. I wasn't Catholic, and though I went to Mass with Ava regularly, I still felt self-conscious about a few things, like kneeling and crossing myself. The Presbyterian in me froze up at those points.

"Ava thinks Antonia was the smart one. The one with the plan." He sighed and rubbed his forehead. "It's true that before—everything happened, with Frankie, Antonia had drive, and Ava was more relaxed. We used to call Ava our laughing girl, did you know that?"

I shook my head, smiling. "No, she's never said that."

He shrugged. "No, she thought she was less because of not being so serious. We never thought that. Frannie and I love all our children. We miss Antonia. Every day, we miss her. But we'd never ask Ava to take her place. She has her own place. The ideas she got, that she had to step into Antonia's shoes, those was her own thinking.

"But still, we're proud of her. She's smart, and she's beautiful. But I worried, because our laughing girl had stopped laughing so much. I told my Frannie that. We talked to her about it, but she only worked all the harder.

"And then . . . she brought you home. And that first weekend, when all she said to us was, 'Oh, Ma, we're just friends—'" Mr. DiMartino's voice took on a high pitch as he imitated his daughter. "We knew. There was something in her face when she talked about you. And we saw how you were with her. How your eyes never left her. How you wanted to be touching her all the time—no, don't worry, I don't mean in a bad way. I mean, you held the door, you touched her shoulder, her arm. We knew. And what made us happy these last few years, Liam, is that we got our laughing girl back. You gave Ava back her laugh."

I blinked back embarrassing moisture in my eyes. Last thing I wanted to do in front of my girlfriend's father was cry like a baby. But Mr. DiMartino didn't seem to notice, or if he did, he didn't care. He pulled me into a strong hug, patted my back three times and then yelled out into the living room.

"Boys! Get in here. We need limoncello. We got something to celebrate."

I smiled now, remembering that day. I'd told them that I was going to wait until after Julia and Jesse's wedding was over. I didn't want to take anything away from their big day, and Ava was so busy with work and with all the wedding prep for her friend that we barely had any time together anyway. But now . . .

I wrapped one of her black curls around my finger. Ava sighed in her sleep and snuggled closer to me. Her fingers found my hand, still resting on her middle, and wove her fingers through mine. Her lips relaxed into a slight smile.

I lay there for another few heartbeats. It was still relatively early; we didn't need to check out until noon, and it was just nine now. I lay my head back down on the pillow and let my eyes drift shut, inhaling deep of the sweet, enticing scent that was uniquely Ava.

"Oh, my God. My head. Ugh." Ava groaned and wriggled away from me. She struggled to sit up, one hand on each temple.

"Lay down, baby. I'll get you some water and ibu." I tossed off the covers and got out of bed.

"I'm not sure I can handle it yet." She put one hand to her stomach. "I just want to sit here for a minute."

I tucked a strand of her hair back behind her ear, frowning. "You didn't even have that much to drink last night."

She shook her head, pressing her lips together. "Too much wine. You know how I get."

"You sure that's all it is?"

Ava's eyes flashed open and rolled at me. "I'm not pregnant, if that's what you mean."

I sat down on the bed and drew her close to my side. "I didn't. Remember, I live with you, babe. I know when things happen. I just meant, do you think you might have a bug or something?"

"I don't think so." She eased herself back onto the pillow and reached to hold my hand. "Might just be the whole week catching up with me."

"I can see that." I traced a circle on the back of her hand. "You just need some down time. Maybe a little more sleep."

"Hmmm. Maybe." She inhaled, deep, and the sheet covering the swell of her breasts slid down a little. I concentrated on not reaching out to touch them. Even lying there, feeling queasy, pale and with her hair spread in a snarled mess on the pillow, Ava was the most beautiful sight in my memory. My heart thudded almost painfully. It was like I was hit all over again by how much I loved this girl. How precious she was to me.

"Babe, can you get me that water now? I think I might be able to keep it down. I need to do something for my head, anyway. It's pounding like a jackhammer."

"Sure." I stood up and dug into my duffle bag for the bottle of ibuprofen. Instead, my fingers closed over that small velvet box. And I knew.

Hands shaking, I found the bottle of pills and stood up to get some water in one of the plastic hotel cups. When I sat back down on the mattress, Ava stretched out both of her hands, eyes still shut.

"Here's the water." I put the cup into her right hand. "And the meds." I dropped one pill on her left palm, and she popped it into her mouth, taking a swig of water and then holding out her hand for the next. I gave it to her and waited while she swallowed it, too. "One more wouldn't hurt."

Ava put out her hand again, but this time, I laid on the black velvet box on it. When she opened her eyes, forehead wrinkling in confusion, I slid off the bed and onto my knee.

Her face was a study in absolute shock. Eyes wide, mouth agape, she stared at the box. I took the cup of water from her other hand and set it on the nightstand. Snagging her right hand in both of mine, I brought it to my lips and kissed the palm.

"What—what's—what're you doing?" She sounded as though she'd been running a marathon.

I licked my lips. My mouth was suddenly dry, and I was

tempted to take a big gulp from her cup of water. And then I looked into her eyes, deep into those beautiful brown eyes that had been my lifeline, my salvation and my temptation. I wasn't nervous anymore.

"Ava Catarine. Since the day I met you, I knew you were someone special. The more I got to know you, the more I liked you. You're kind, funny, loyal and so smart you scare the shit out of me half the time.

"And you're beautiful. God, so beautiful. More than you'll ever realize, because you don't see it. Sometimes I look up at you, when we're studying at night or when you're cooking . . . or when we're riding in the car, and you're singing along with Frank . . . and I think, my God. What wonderful thing did I ever do to deserve this girl in my life? The answer is nothing. I don't deserve you, but like we always say, I'm keeping you anyway."

Tears had pooled in her eyes, and now they spilled over down her cheeks as her bottom lip trembled.

"Ava, you saved my life. Before you . . . I was barely surviving. I was getting by. But nothing mattered to me. I did what my parents expected. I pretended to be someone I hated. I was the jerk and the asshole you all thought I was."

"And then you . . . you saw me. You looked at me, and you told me I could be more. You believed in me. When you did that, when you touched me and loved me, I believed in me, too. I knew that as long as you were with me, believing in me, I could do anything in the world."

Ava drew in a ragged breath and raised our joined hands to brush tears from her face.

"All I want for the rest of my life is to be with you. To belong to you, and to know that you belong to me. I don't care what else happens, as long as I have that. As long as I have you. You are my life. Let me be yours. Marry me, Ava. Be my forever."

My hands still shaking, I took the box from where it still

sat on her left palm, and I opened it. Ava's eyes widened, and she bit down on her bottom lip. I watched, my heart pounding, while she raised her gaze to mine and the most beautiful smile I've ever seen spread across her face before she whispered the only word I wanted to hear.

"Yes."

"I CAN'T BELIEVE YOU proposed to me while I looked like this." Ava laughed, standing in front of the mirror. "I'm hung over, yesterday's makeup is smeared across my face, and my hair looks like a bird's nest."

I stood behind her and wrapped my arms around her waist. "You've never looked more beautiful to me."

"Which goes to show how crazy you are." She turned in my arms and kissed my chin. "And tells me that you really must love me, because you'd have to be blind in love to ask me to spend the rest of my life with you, looking like this."

"I do, and I am." I gave her a light smack on the ass and began to get ready for a shower.

"This is the most beautiful ring I've ever seen." Ava held up her hand to the light, turning it to let the diamond sparkle. "I love the round diamond."

"There's some history in the ring." I stripped off my T-shirt and took her hand, kissing the tips of her fingers. "The main diamond . . . it was my grandmother's. My granddad, the one who liked old time movies? He left me Gramma's ring. I had the stone reset, and then I was talking to your mom one day, and she told me she had a ring that belonged to *her* grandmother. We took the small accents from that one and added them to this ring. So it's a combination of our families. Of us."

"Oh, my God, Liam, that's . . . that's the most wonderful

thing—wait. My mom? You talked to my mom about engagement rings?"

I grinned, smug. "Yup. And your dad, too."

She swatted my shoulder, and I dodged. "When was that?"

I shrugged. "Earlier this spring. Right after I asked for your father's blessing."

Ava sat down on the edge of the bed. "Just when I think I've got you figured out, Liam Bailey, you blow my me away. Again. Here I was thinking you'd changed your mind about ever getting married."

I turned on the water in the shower and then poked my head around the corner of the bathroom door to look at her curiously. "Why'd you think that?"

She pulled her knees up to her chin, a classic Ava-pose. "You stopped talking about it. I figured with everything going on between your mom and dad . . ." Her voice trailed off.

"Yeah, well, that played into it, but I never changed my mind. I planned to ask you before, but I didn't want our engagement tangled up with my parents' mess. When I realized that wasn't going to end any time soon, I decided I wasn't going to let them interfere with our lives."

Ava smiled, those sweet lips curving up and her eyes shining so that I wanted to grab her and take her back to bed. I glanced over her shoulder at the digital clock next to the bed. *Damn.* It was too close to check-out time.

"I'm glad you decided that. Did my parents know you were going to propose this weekend?"

I smiled and shook my head. "No. I didn't exactly plan this out. I had another idea, but this morning just felt . . . right. Like it was the best time." I snagged a towel off the rack.

"So I guess we better call them on the way home. Mom'll freak out if I don't let her know right away."

"I might have a better idea. Why don't we just swing down there? It's Sunday, the restaurant's closed. We could tell them in person."

Ava's whole face lit up. "Really? We could do that?"

Making this girl glow like she was right now was my goal every single day. Knowing it was as easy today as a little side trip made my heart swell. "Sure. It's just about twenty minutes out of the way. Why not?"

"NOW LISTEN . . . WHEN WE get to my parents' house, they're going to ask a lot of questions. About our plans for the wedding, when we want to have it, where we want to have it . . . don't let them bulldoze you, okay? We're going to stick to the party line."

I quirked a half-smile at Ava. Sitting in the passenger seat of the Beemer, her feet under her and knees curled to the side, she looked about as intimidating as a baby kitten. But I'd seen my girl get her dander up, and I knew she was a force to be reckoned with.

"Okay. But what's the party line, exactly?"

She held up one finger, and then another, ticking them off. "We just got engaged today. We're going to enjoy *being* engaged for a while. We'll make plans in our own time. And we'll be the ones making the decisions, without any pressure from anyone else."

"Aye-aye, captain." I sketched a salute. "And how do you think that's going to fly with the general?"

Ava stuck out her tongue at me. "First of all, you're mixing both your metaphors and your branches of service. Second, if by the general you mean my mother—" She swallowed and set her jaw. "I'll take her on."

I whistled under my breath. "I think I'll just duck and stay out of the line of fire."

She laughed. "Probably a good idea." She pulled her knees

up and rested her chin on top of them. "My mom means well. But I'm her only daughter." A shadow fell across her face, and I knew she was thinking about her sister, Antonia. They'd been so close, and even though Antonia had been gone for seven years, Ava still missed her. Reaching across, I took hold of her hand.

"Hey. You know we can do this however you want." I struggled for a minute with what I needed to say versus what I really wanted. "Do you think you want a big wedding?"

Ava made a face. "Right now, after seeing everything that went into Julia's huge shindig? I want to run in the opposite direction. I'm thinking you, me, my parents and yours—"

I stiffened a little. "I'm with you until the part where you said my parents. I want them kept far away from this. From us."

"Liam, I understand how you feel about them. But they're still your parents, and I think in the long run, you'll wish you had them at your wedding." She gripped my hand a little tighter and fixed me with that steely-Ava gaze. "Even if you don't believe me right now."

"It's not that I don't believe you. And maybe I would regret it, eventually. But right now, seeing them, telling them we're getting married . . . it's the last thing I want to do."

Ava bit the side of her lip. "Well, we can table that discussion for now. One mountain at a time. But like I was saying, I don't want a big wedding." She slanted a look at me. "Unless you do."

"Babe, I just want to marry you. In a church, on a ship, in a courthouse—wherever it happens, I don't care. As long as it happens."

She rose up on her knees and leaned across to kiss my cheek. My upper arm brushed against her breasts, and I felt the familiar stirring between my legs. I loved that my girl never failed to turn me on, no matter what.

"So we've worked out that we don't care how. But not too big or over the top. What about when?" Ava sank back onto her seat.

"As soon as possible." That was an answer that I didn't have to think about. "I'd put another ring on your finger today if we could."

"I feel the same. Although would you think I'm hopelessly corny if I told you I'd always wanted a Christmas wedding?"

"Really?" I checked out the rearview mirror and changed lanes. "Nah, not corny, but why Christmas? Don't most girls want a June wedding?"

"I'm not most girls." She winked at me. "I don't know. One of my cousins got married during the holidays when I was really little, and I remember thinking the church was so pretty, all decorated with evergreens and the tree."

"So you do want to get married in the church."

Ava looked surprised for a minute, and then she laughed. "I guess I do. I hadn't thought about it, but whenever I picture myself getting married, it's in the church. Or *a* church, at least." She frowned. "Does that bother you?"

"No." Although I'd been raised Presbyterian, my family had really only gone to church when my father needed us to look good for a campaign. Ava was undoubtedly more devout. "Do I have to do anything special? Like . . . a ritual bathing or something?"

She sighed. "Liam, have you been watching *Sex and the City* again? No, Charlotte was converting to Judaism, not Catholicism. I'm not sure of the whole process, but we can talk to Father Byers."

I'd met the priest, who was a long-time friend of the DiMartino family. He was now rector of Our Lady of Mercy, the Catholic church just off the Birch University campus, and I sometimes accompanied Ava to Mass on Saturday nights. He seemed pretty cool . . . for a priest.

"Did you call your mom and tell her we were coming?" I slowed to merge onto the exit ramp for Seagrove City.

"No. You know Mom. She'd immediately think something

horrible had happened, or that we were coming to tell them bad news. I texted with her before we left, though, just to say hello, and she said they were planning to stay home all day and do yard work. So they should be there."

I followed the route that was so familiar to me now, through the winding two-lane roads, with dunes and sea reeds on one side and tall pine trees on the other. We passed by Cucina Felice, looking empty and forlorn today with its empty parking lot and dark windows.

The DiMartinos lived in a modest house on a quiet street about five minutes from the family restaurant. As soon as we turned the corner, I spotted Mrs. DiMartino in the front yard, wearing a wide straw hat as she knelt among her flowers. She turned as I pulled into the driveway, and true to her daughter's prediction, I saw a flash of panicked surprise cross her face.

Ava squeezed my hand one more time. "Ready to face the music, lover? Gird up your loins."

"Hey, my loins are always ready. Bring it. I'm not afraid of your family. Much. Anymore."

She laughed and opened the car door.

"Ava, what in the world are you doing here? What's wrong? What happened?" Mrs. DiMartino tugged off her gardening gloves as she approached us.

"Ma, always with the jumping to the worst conclusions. Geez. Where's Daddy?"

"He's inside with Frankie, watching the ball game. Why?"

The front door opened, and a small dark-haired tornado spun out, followed by Ava's father. "I thought I heard a car pull in. Hiya, honey. Hey, Liam."

Frankie, Ava's seven-year old niece, threw herself against my knees. "Liam! I didn't know you were coming today!"

"None of us did. I thought you were at Julia's wedding." Mrs. DiMartino was still tense, waiting for the proverbial other shoe to drop.

"We were. But . . . ." Ave glanced at me as I bent to scoop

Frankie up into my arms. "We had good news that we want to tell you in person." She held up her hand, and the ring glinted in the bright summer sunshine. "We're engaged."

"Oh. Oh, Ava!" Her mother dropped the small hoe she'd been holding and her gloves and snatched at her daughter's hand. "Let me see. Oh, thank God . . . it looks so beautiful on your hand."

"Yeah, aren't you the sneaky one." Ava pulled her hand back and hugged her mom. "You knew. And you didn't even give me a hint."

I watched Mrs. DiMartino's face as she embraced Ava. Her eyes were closed, but a suspicious moisture had gathered at the corners. "Why's that such a surprise? I can keep a secret."

"Stop hogging her, Frannie. Let a father have a turn." Mr. DiMartino's face relaxed into a smile as he held his little girl. "This is a happy day. We're so glad for you, Ava." He reached out an arm and pulled me into the hug. "Liam. So happy."

"Nonna, why is everyone hugging?" Frankie looked from her grandmother to her aunt. "Auntie Ave, what's on your hand?"

Ava came to stand next to me, holding her fingers up to the little girl. "It's a ring, Frankie. Liam gave it to me." She glanced at me, her eyes shining. "We're getting married."

Frankie's small forehead wrinkled. "So you're going to have a wedding? Do I get to be a flower girl again? Like when Uncle Carl and Auntie Ange had their wedding?"

Ava's gaze met mine over the little girl's head. No way in hell I was going to tell her that she couldn't put on a princess dress and walk down the aisle. I was one of Frankie's favorites, and I wasn't going to mess that up.

"Well, sweetie, we'll have to see. Liam and I probably aren't having a wedding just like Carl and Angela."

Her parents had already started into the house, but Mrs. DiMartino stopped abruptly and turned around. "What do you mean by that?"

"Let's go inside and talk, Frannie. Come on." Ava's dad turned and smiled at me. "The boys are coming over in a little while for dinner. Can you stay? I'll open a bottle of prosecco and we'll celebrate."

I held the door with my free hand and let Ava go in ahead of Frankie and me. When she glanced back at me with eyebrows raised, I nodded. "Fine with me. I'm on break from both classes and work at the university for the next week. It's up to Ava. She's the one who has to get up and go into the agency tomorrow."

"How often do you get engaged? Only the once. We need to celebrate." Mrs. DiMartino's voice was firm.

Ava smiled. "Okay, sure. But we can't stay too late. I haven't been home for a week, and I've got to be ready to go back to work."

For the next fifteen minutes, typical DiMartino bedlam ensued. I sat back watching, amused, while Ava told her parents about how I'd proposed—or at least, she told them a sanitized, parent-friendly version, wherein we were having breakfast at the hotel restaurant when I'd popped the question. Although the whole family knew that Ava and I'd been living together for nearly two years, her parents chose not to look too closely at that situation. I think Mrs. DiMartino comforted herself that since we had two bedrooms, there was at least a chance that we weren't sleeping together.

And then Carl and Angela arrived, and shortly after, Vincent, and we had to go through everything all over again. Angela, being very nearly nine months pregnant, burst into tears, throwing both her husband and her mother-in-law into a panic. Everyone fussed around her for a few minutes, until she waved them away.

"Stop it! I'm fine. These are happy tears. Ava, I'm so glad for you. We're going to have a blast, planning your wedding."

Mr. DiMartino was passing tall flutes of bubbling white wine around the room. His wife leaned over to squeeze Ava's shoulder. "Yes, we are. What are you thinking, Ava? Next summer? Next spring? What colors do you want to use? And we'll need to figure out the engagement party and the shower, so they don't interfere with the baby's christening." She nodded toward Ange.

"Ma, slow down. We just got engaged today. We're not sure what we want to do yet. Give us some time, okay?" Ava softened the words with a smile and a hand on her mom's arm.

"What's there to decide? This is how you do things. You get the ring, you put the announcement in the paper, you have a party. You pick a date, you find a place to have it. Then we choose a dress, you take your bridesmaids shopping. You register for gifts. We throw a shower. You talk to the priest. We have a wedding, and you get married."

It took a strong woman to stand up to Francesca DiMartino, but my girl was that woman. She drew up her small body and fastened her mother with a stern look.

"Mom, stop. Give us time. Can't we just be happy today, and enjoy each other, and then worry about the other stuff later?"

There was a long moment of absolute silence in the living room. Even little Frankie didn't move. Mr. DiMartino was the first one to speak.

"Frannie, she's right. Let's be happy for today. Look, we've got all our family around us. We'll celebrate tonight, because we have something wonderful to look forward to. And we're getting a new son. Everything else will take care of itself." He gazed around the room, a broad smile on his face. "Now, who's ready to help me in the kitchen? The macaroni isn't going to cook itself."

Chapter Four

Ava

"WELCOME BACK, AVA. HOW was your vacation?" Suzanne, my boss, wandered into my small office and dropped into a chair across from my desk. She brushed back a strand of her dark brown hair, cut in a classic long bob so that it fell in a silky curtain around her impeccably made-up face.

"It wasn't much of a vacation. I was in a wedding on Saturday, and so I spent the whole week at the bride's house, getting ready for the big day."

"Ugh." She wrinkled her small nose. "The entire week? You used your vacation days for that?"

I sighed. "Yeah, she's a really good friend. She had little parties or get-togethers scheduled every single day leading up to the wedding itself. I couldn't miss any of them."

"You're a much nicer person than me. I've been in weddings . . . and I don't think I would've been able to stomach a full week of it."

"Well, I'm back now. I checked on all the campaigns as

much as I could while I was away, and it looks like Tanya did a good job maintaining the postings. I'm going to jump on the new clients' accounts today, unless you've got anything else for me."

"No, that sounds good. You're going to have to create most of the accounts for that gym client, by the way. The guy is a social media moron. Oh, and before I forget, didn't you tell me you had a friend who's an event planner? There's a new boutique opening here in town, and they hired us to promote their grand opening. Our usual planner is booked already."

"Sure. Giff Mackay. He's amazing . . . he did the wedding I went to this weekend. Hold on, I'll get you his contact info." I reached for my cell, but before I could grab it, Suzanne gasped and jumped up.

"Ava! What's that on your finger?" She clutched my left hand, holding it up and staring at the ring. "Oh my God, it's gorgeous."

"Thanks." My face warmed. I didn't understand why this embarrassed me, but it did.

"Does it mean what I think it does? Liam finally popped the question?" She let go of my hand and sat back down.

"Finally? What's that supposed to mean?"

Suzanne shrugged. "I don't know. You've been together since college. You've lived together for two years, right? Just seems like it's long past time you two'd make it legal."

"I never thought you were that big a fan of marriage." I'd known Suzanne since my internship here at the ad agency, and as far as I was aware, she'd never had a boyfriend. She dated, but never the same guy for more than a few weeks.

"Not for me, I'm not, but you . . ." She smiled. "Ava, when I first saw you with Liam, I knew how it was. You two belong together. You're a walking ad for happily ever after."

That should've made me glow, but it almost felt like a put-down. "It doesn't mean I'm less serious about my job. Yes, I'm getting married, but it won't change how much I work or make me lose my focus."

"Whoa." Suzanne held up her hand. "No one said anything about that. Ava, I'm thrilled for you. You know how Margaret runs this business. Her motto is that happy workers make happy clients. Liam makes you happy. I'm not asking you to apologize for that, any more than I'll make excuses for not being in a relationship."

I leaned back in my chair. "Sorry. I guess I might be a little defensive. We only got engaged about twenty-four hours ago, and I spent last evening with my family. My mom wants to plan this huge wedding, and no one can understand why I don't want it. No one but Liam, that is. And when I pointed out to my mother that I have a job, that I can't just devote my life to being a bride, she doesn't seem to get it. It's like putting on this ring teleported me back to 1955."

Suzanne shook her head. "It doesn't have to mean that. Stand your ground, but remember, your parents love you, and that's why they want to celebrate this. Don't let it get to you." She stood up and shot me a grin. "Although it does remind me why I prefer footloose and fancy-free. Oh, and just text me that information for the event planner, please."

I watched Suzanne leave the office, her expensive heels clicking on the wooden floor. Rubbing my forehead, I sagged back, closing my eyes. It wasn't even noon, and I was already exhausted.

Liam and I had managed to get out of my parents' house the night before without committing to anything related to wedding planning. I'd slept all the way home, and when we'd gotten there, I'd stripped off my clothes and fallen into bed, completely forgetting to set my alarm. Consequently, this morning I'd woken with just enough time to take a quick shower and dress for work.

All of which had gone into making me a very grumpy fiancée. Liam, knowing me by now, had stayed out of my way and pressed a to-go cup of coffee into my hand as I raced by him toward the door.

"I love you. I'll see you tonight." I tossed the words over my shoulder as I hustled my way to the car.

I was so focused on getting to the office and then in seeing what I'd missed during my week off that I honestly forgot all about the ring on my finger until Suzanne pointed it out. So now I was not only filled with a swirl of feelings related to being engaged, but I was also flooded with guilt about forgetting that I *was* engaged.

The answer to all those emotions was clearly to bury myself in work and avoid thinking about them at all. And that was exactly what I did, keeping my hands on the keyboard and my eyes on the computer screen, working through lunch and not looking up until the buzzing of my phone caught my attention.

I rolled my eyes when my mother's picture flashed across the caller ID. For a moment, I toyed with the idea of ignoring the call. After all, she knew I was at work. It annoyed me that she was okay with interrupting that.

But in the end, daughter guilt overcame righteous indignation, and I answered.

"Hey, Ma, what's up?"

"Ava, I'm sorry to bother you at work." I winced. *So she wasn't completely unaware.* "But I didn't want to disturb Liam, and I need his mother's phone number."

I raised one eyebrow, as though she could see me. "Didn't you hear Liam say he's off this week? What were you going to disturb?"

Her tongue click sounded clear through the phone. "You know men, Ava, they always have something going on. I'm sure he's busy. Anyway, just give me Mrs. Bailey's number, and I'll let you get back to whatever you were doing."

"Why do you need her number?" The idea of my mother and Liam's chatting just didn't sit well. The two women had met at our college graduation two years ago, and they'd gotten along without any issue. But that was before the Baileys had split up, and before I was about to be Laura Bailey's daughter-in-law.

Daughter-in-law. The words made my stomach clench. I had no problem with the idea of being Liam's wife. I loved that. But although his parents and I had come to a sort of peace over the last few years, I still wasn't comfortable with them. I was fairly certain the feeling was mutual.

"Your father and I want to invite them to dinner. Liam's parents, I mean. So we can talk about the wedding plans. It's how things are done, Ava. The bride's parents call the groom's parents, and they work it all out between them."

"No, no, no." I gritted my teeth and got up to close my office door. "Listen, Ma, I get that you're excited and you want to start making this a big deal, but you can't. Not yet. Maybe not at all. We haven't even told Liam's parents that we're engaged."

"Why on earth not?" My mother's voice went up three octaves. I heard a shout behind her amid the sound of other voices, and I realized she must be in the kitchen at the restaurant.

"Because he's not ready. You don't know how they are, Ma. They're not like us. The whole family's messed up. His dad is banging his secretary, and maybe someone else, too. We don't know. And his mom is dating her yoga teacher, and they both want to tell Liam all about it—"

"Ava Catarine! Stop. I don't want to hear this, God forbid, and watch your language. I'm sorry about Liam's parents. Divorce is always a tragedy. But he has to tell them. Don't you think they're going to figure it out when they get the wedding invitation?"

"If they do." I stretched back in my chair and let it swivel in a slow circle. "We still don't know what kind of wedding we're having, Ma. Maybe we'll just do it and then tell them afterward. Eventually."

There was an ominous silence on the other end of the line. The background noise swelled and then faded, and I heard a sharp bang that sounded like a door slamming. Yeah, she was pissed, and she'd taken this conversation outside so she could yell at me in peace.

"Ava, this is your wedding. The one and only you'll ever have. You don't 'just do it' and then tell the groom's parents. That's not how we do things."

"Maybe it's not how Carl and Angela did, but Liam and I are different. We want. . well, we're not sure exactly what we want yet, but not a huge affair."

The sigh my mother heaved nearly stirred my hair, even from sixty miles away. "I just don't understand. I thought you always wanted a fairy tale wedding. Is it Liam? Does he want it quieter?"

"Actually, Ma, no. I was the one who told him I thought I wanted something smaller. I saw what Julia and Jesse went through. And . . ." I rubbed the side of my neck. "It was hard enough on them with Jesse's mom being a crazy lady. *Both* of Liam's parents are acting like children. It would just eat at him, having to get through a big wedding with them sniping at each other. And us."

"Okay." Her voice was resigned. "But you still need to tell them about that you're engaged. Remember, Ava, these two people are going to be part of your life from now on. This isn't just about a wedding. It's about a marriage."

"I hear you, Ma. Thanks." I glanced at the clock on my computer screen. "Listen, I need to go. I have a meeting in five minutes. I'll talk to you later. Love you."

"Love you, too, sweetie. Think about what I said."

I WAS SERIOUSLY DRAGGING when I got home that night. As I pulled into the parking lot of our complex, I passed Giff and Jeff's corner-unit townhouse and spotted them sitting on the deck. When Giff recognized my car, he jumped up and waved his arms.

I stopped at the curb and rolled down my window. "Hey, good looking. Are you guys grilling tonight?"

"Yeah, we're doing the barbecue deal, but let's talk about something more important. Gimme." He held out his hand, motioning to me.

Grinning, I played dumb. "What do you mean? Give you what?"

"Don't play with me, peaches! I want to see that sparkler my boy put on your finger."

"Okay, but don't touch. You're going to be totally jealous." I laid my hand on his palm.

"Oh, look at this. Jeff, come here. Check out what these two crazy kids have gone and done."

Jeff strolled over and bent to look in the window, resting one arm over Giff's back. "Hey, Ava. Congratulations are in order, huh? That's great. Did the wedding this weekend inspire you?"

I laughed. "Actually, I think Liam showed great courage proposing when he did. Not that you didn't do an amazing job, Giff. You did. Just a lot to take in, I guess."

"I'm so happy for you both." Giff swallowed hard, and I felt a lump in my own throat. He'd been such a good friend to both of us. Without Giff's intervention, I might've been too stubborn to take a chance on Liam. I couldn't imagine what my life would've been like today if I hadn't, but it would be far emptier.

"Did Liam tell you?" I craned my neck to see them better.

"Yeah, we went to the gym this morning. He was bursting with the news." He released my hand and tapped the side of the car. "I know you're on your way home now, but just give me a shout when you're ready to start planning. We'll sit down and look at dates, venues . . . I can't wait."

Oddly, the idea of disappointing Giff by telling him we

weren't having a huge wedding weighed on me more than the thought of upsetting my mom. "Well . . . it's early days yet. We'll see."

Giff cocked one eyebrow at me. "Beetle said something about Christmas. If you're talking *this* Christmas, peaches, we're already behind times."

I shrugged and repeated my last words. "We'll see." I leaned down and smiled up at both of them. "I'll let you get back to your grilling. See you later."

"You can count on it. Remember what I said. Tick-tock, tick-tock."

I stuck out my tongue at him and drove away.

Our townhouse was several buildings down, and by the time I parked and climbed the few stairs to our front door, my head was beginning to pound. But as soon as I stepped inside, a tempting aroma wafted to my nose. Liam met me with a kiss and a glass of wine.

I wound my arms around his neck. "You are without doubt the best boyfriend in the world. Hey, want to marry me?"

He rubbed his nose against mine, smiling. "I think I just might do that." He kissed me again, this time a simple touch to my lips. "Why don't you go get changed? I've got enchiladas in the oven, and they should be ready by the time you come downstairs."

"You know, if this history professor gig doesn't work out, you could just be a house husband." I called the words back as I headed upstairs. "I like coming home to a hot supper."

"I'll keep that in mind. Hurry up, before it's not hot anymore."

In our room, I was further delighted to see that he'd also unpacked the suitcases and done all the laundry. I changed as fast as I could, since my stomach was reminding me that I'd missed lunch today.

"Here you go. Sit down, and I'll bring the food." Liam pulled out my chair for me.

"Okay. So you did the laundry, cleaned the house, set the table and made dinner. Is there something you have to tell me?" I picked up my wine glass and sipped.

"Yes, as a matter of fact, there is." He set the long glass dish of enchiladas in the center of the table and squatted down next to my chair. Brushing back my hair from my face, he smiled. "Thank you for saying yes. All day long, I kept thinking . . . I can't believe how lucky I am. I get to spend the rest of my life with you."

Tears sprung to my eyes. "I'm the luckiest." I smoothed my fingers over his cheek. "How many girls get the hot guy they never dreamed of having . . . and then it turns out he's also a wonderful cook, too?"

Liam laughed as he stood up. "Don't forget great in bed."

I reached to spoon food onto my plate. "Don't worry. I could never forget that." I forked off a bite of enchilada. "Mmmm . . . this is delicious."

"Good." We ate in silence for a few moments before he spoke again. "How was your first day back at work? Was it crazy?"

"Not as bad as it could've been, I guess." I set down my fork and wiped my lips with the napkin. "Suzanne loved my ring. Oh, and my mom called. She wanted your mother's phone number."

Liam froze mid-bite. "Why?"

"Why else? Wedding planning. Don't worry." I laid a hand on his arm. "I didn't give her the number, and I told her we'd take care of everything in our own time."

He relaxed a bit, his shoulders sagging. "Okay, thanks." He finished the last morsel on his plate and leaned back. "You know, if it weren't for your family, I'd say we should just fly to Vegas and get married. Or . . . some island. Keep it simple. And then just tell my parents after it's a done deal."

"My mother said today that we need to remember this isn't just our wedding, it's our marriage. That we can't ignore your mother and father for the rest of our lives."

"I don't know. It's worth a try." Liam's smile was weak, and then he groaned. "Okay, yeah, she's right. I'll call them. Before the end of the week."

"Sounds good." I drained my wine glass. "In other news, Giff seems happy for us. I didn't have the heart to tell him we wouldn't need him to plan it, since we're keeping everything small."

"Uh . . ." Liam averted his eyes. "Well, couldn't he still set it up, even if it we don't go over the top? I might've told him today that we'd have him run the show."

I stood up to carry my plate to the sink. "You're a pushover, Liam Bailey. I can see that I can't leave you alone with my mother from now on. She'll have you agreeing to a ceremony at the Vatican and reception on the QEII. And between both Giff and my mom . . . everything would be out of control."

"I just hate to disappoint Giff. And when I told him about us getting engaged, he was so happy. He assumed he'd be the wedding planner, and I didn't want to hurt his feelings."

"Hey, it's fine with me. Just don't complain when things spiral out of our control. It's all on your head."

I LOVED HAVING LIAM at home while I worked. He made me breakfast and coffee to go every morning and had dinner and a glass of wine waiting every night. He even drove to Haddonfield to meet me for lunch one day. I hid a smile as my female co-workers' eyes glazed over, watching him stroll into the office. He wore faded jeans and a polo in the exact same blue of his eyes, and the way he moved . . . he was like sex on wheels. Or Vans, more accurately. When he pushed open my office door, his face came alive with that slow-burn of a smile.

He leaned over my desk to kiss me.

"Hey, beautiful. Ready for lunch?"

What I was ready for had nothing to do with eating. I was wracking my brain for a hotel nearby where we could rent a room for an hour. I gripped his shirt and pulled him back down to me again.

The kiss was just getting really interesting when I heard someone in the doorway clearing her throat.

"You have a visitor, Ava?" There was a mischievous humor in Suzanne's voice.

"Hey, Suzanne. Good to see you." Liam leaned against my desk and grinned at my boss. "I'm going to steal my girl here for lunch, if that's okay."

"Of course it is. She's been killing herself all week, catching up. Take her away, and don't let her answer the phone, check social media or talk work at all." She fastened me with her stern look. "Shoo."

"Okay, okay, I'm shooing." I unhooked my handbag from the back of my chair. "I can just stay out all afternoon, if that'd make you feel better."

"Works for me." Liam slung his arm around my shoulder.

"Ha, you two are so funny. No, bring her back. I want to wring as much good out of her as I can before she transforms into bridezilla."

"Hey." I cocked my head, insulted. "I'm not going to turn into bridezilla."

"Yeah, so you say. You won't mean to do it. Right now, you think you've got this under control, but once you start looking at wedding gowns and tasting cake, it'll take over your life. I've seen it happen, darling."

"Not to me. I'm capable of compartmentalizing my life. Right?" I appealed to Liam, one eyebrow raised.

"More than anyone I've ever met." He slid his hand down my arm to lace his fingers through mine. "Don't worry, Suzanne. We're keeping everything quiet. I promise, no wedding craziness here."

"See, that's what drives me nuts," I told Liam as we sat at a small table at our favorite bistro. It was a nice enough day to eat alfresco, and I was enjoying the sunshine. "People see me with a ring on my finger, and they assume I'm going to lose my mind, stop doing my job and turn into some Frankenbride. But does anyone expect *you* to change? Has anyone asked you if you've thought about your tux? Or what colors we plan to use? Or if you're planning to take time off? No. Just me."

Liam dragged a French fry through ketchup. "Yeah, I get that it's not fair. But what are you going to do, except just prove them wrong by not going crazy?" He grinned at me, leaning forward. "I believe in you. And just so you know, if you start acting like—what did you call it? Frankenbride? I'll be happy to give you the wake-up call. I'll stage an intervention."

I stuck out my tongue at him.

By Friday—less than a week post-proposal—I'd fielded seven phone calls from my mother asking for updates, five texts from Giff sending me potential reception sites and two emails from my sister-in-law Angela with links to bridesmaid dresses she liked. I'd ignored everything I could, pacified and put off what I could not, and I was done. When a post came across my social media feed advertising a special price on a flight to Vegas, my finger itched to one-click that baby. It'd serve them all right.

I turned off my phone and shoved it deep into my handbag before I drove back to the townhouse that night. Somehow my mom seemed to sense when I was on my way home; that was her favorite time to call. I was hoping that it being Friday night—one of the busiest times at the restaurant—would keep her occupied. For now, at least.

Liam had suggested going out to dinner that night, and I was looking forward to an evening of good food, some wine and then heading back home for hot Friday night sex. I smiled in anticipation, thinking maybe I'd dig out his favorite short black skirt to wear tonight. It'd been his favorite when we were first dating, and even now, it drove him wild when I wore it. Thinking about it and remembering his hands on me sent a thrill of desire down my middle. So maybe we'd start with the hot Friday night sex and have a late dinner.

I opened the front door and called up the steps. "Hey, baby. I'm home. Are you naked? I think we should have a special appetizer before we go to dinner." I stepped out of my shoes and moved toward the kitchen, hopping on one foot to pull off my black stockings as I went. "You know, the type that involves getting sweaty between the sheets—oh."

I stopped abruptly just inside the kitchen, my pantyhose wadded up in one hand. Liam was sitting at our small round table, and he wasn't alone. His mother was in the chair across from him.

Every word I'd shouted since I'd walked in the door reverberated in my brain and made me want to sink through the floor. Liam's mouth was tense, but I caught flickers of amusement in his eyes.

"Uh—sorry, I didn't know—um, hi, Mrs. Bailey." I threw Liam a panicked glance. *Fuck. What the hell was his mother doing here?*

"Hello, Ava. How are you, dear?" Laura Bailey pasted a smile on her face. She looked nearly as upset as her son. I noticed that she'd cut her hair, and that while it was usually almost the same shade of Liam's, it now appeared a shade or two blonder.

"What's going on?" I stuffed my stockings into my purse and hung it on a chair. "I mean, this is a surprise. Right?" I was pretty sure I'd remember if we knew she was coming to see us.

"Yes, it is. As a matter of fact, quite a few *surprises* seem to be going around, don't they?" Mrs. Bailey looked pointedly at my left hand.

"Oh." I sat down and stuck my hand under the table, as though I could undo knowledge by hiding the ring. "How

. . . did you just come down to visit Liam?"

Liam shook his head grimly. "She heard . . . through the grapevine. Giff told his mom, and then she ran into my mother at . . . uh, yoga class."

I held onto my smile. "Oh, okay. Well . . ." I wasn't sure how to fix this situation, particularly as I was walking into it blind. I had no idea what Liam had told his mother before I got home.

"I told Mom that we just wanted a little time to keep the news to ourselves." He rescued me, and I flashed him a grateful smile.

"Exactly. We had Julia and Jesse's wedding last week, and then I had to get back to work Monday. We've been so busy." It sounded lame, even to my ears, and by the way Mrs. Bailey's mouth puckered, I had the feeling she was hearing it the same way.

"I've been trying to call my son since last week. I finally drove down here, hoping I might catch him. I'd planned to just camp out on your front step until one of you got home." She glanced at Liam. "Happily for me, he was home when I got here."

I wished with all my might for a glass of wine. Or maybe even something a little stronger. Beneath the table, I twisted my hands together.

"Mom, I'm not going to lie to you." Liam ran a hand through his hair. "I've been avoiding both you and Dad because talking to either of you isn't much fun these days. Dad wants to harp on me about the opportunities I'm missing, and you want to tell me about how great your new life is. Sorry. I don't want to hear it."

Laura Bailey shifted in her chair. "You're an adult, Liam. If you're old enough to be getting married—" Her eye twitched. "—then I think you're old enough to be responsible and return telephone calls. And . . . I think you need to know too that you've hurt me. Can you imagine how I felt, running into

Melinda Mackay and having her fuss over your news? And me completely ignorant? I played it off, but she knew. I was mortified."

"I'm sure neither of us meant—" I tried a placating tone, faltering when she swung her gaze toward me.

"Have you told *your* parents yet, Ava?"

I locked eyes with Liam. *Shit.* I wasn't going to lie, but this had huge ugly potential. "Um, well, yeah, we did."

"Mom, you know what? Yeah, we told the DiMartinos. Matter of fact, we drove down to see them Sunday to tell them in person. Because if you want adult-sized honesty, *Mother,* Ava's parents have been more like family to me than you and Dad ever have. It was my idea to go talk to her parents, because they've taken me in like I'm one of them. Neither you or Dad have done that for Ava. You treat her like she's a passing fad in my life. Well, I told you before and I'll tell you again. She's here to stay. I love her, she's going to be my wife, and if you can't get accept that fact, then you can both just leave us alone." Liam stood up and shoved his chair under the table. His teeth were clenched, and I watched his jaw work. I didn't think I'd seen him this angry for a very long time.

"Liam, please. Enough melodrama. You're making it sound like I don't like Ava." Mrs. Bailey turned luminous eyes on me. "Of course I do. She's a lovely girl, and I think you're both going to be very happy." She lifted one shoulder. "Now what your father says or how he acts . . . that's a different story. You know how judgmental and critical he is."

Liam closed his eyes and shook his head. "Don't start, Mom. This isn't an opportunity for you to make Dad look bad."

She sniffed. "Doesn't take much. I wonder which of his bimbos he'll bring as his date to your wedding. The secretary, or the aid? Or who knows who else he's . . . seeing."

I jumped in to save Liam from having to do it. "Actually, Mrs. Bailey, we might not even be having a wedding. I mean, we're getting married, but we just want to do something quiet.

Maybe just immediate family. Very small."

Liam's mother looked as though she'd smelled something very unpleasant. "Why on earth would you do that? Weddings are meant to be celebrations. Not quiet little dinner parties, unless it's a second marriage for both or unless—" Realization dawned on her face, and she glanced at me, her eyes dropping to my waist. "Oh. Are you . . ."

"No. God, Mom."

She held up her hands. "It happens. I mean, you've been living together for two years. You wouldn't be the first couple to put the cart before the horse. It seems like these days more people have the baby before the honeymoon. I wasn't judging, I was just asking."

"Well, now you've got your answer." Liam stood with his hands on his hips. "We haven't made up our mind what kind of wedding we're having or even when we're having it. When we do, we'll let you know."

"Will you?" Mrs. Bailey stood up, too, facing her son. "Or will I have to hear about it from Giff's mother again? Or maybe read it in the newspaper? Oh, I have an even better idea. Why don't you tell your father about it, and he can have one of his whores give me a call, just like she did when I found about his lying, cheating ass?"

My mouth dropped, and I was sure my eyes were wide as saucers. Laura Bailey never swore. She never used vulgar words; as a matter of fact, I was fairly certain I'd never even heard her say 'darn.' Over the past year, she'd turned passive-aggressive into an art form, but always with a smile on her face and with perfectly correct language. I bit my lip. *She must really be pissed.*

"Mom. No. We'll call you, I promise." He glanced at me. "As a matter of fact, why don't we all get together next week? We can talk about everything then. Ava's parents, you and Dad . . . okay?"

She sighed, her eyes boring into the floor and her lips

pressed tight. I had the sense that she was holding herself together by the thinnest of threads. Finally, she nodded. "Fine. When?"

I jumped in. "Sunday? The restaurant's closed, and we could . . . just have everyone come here for brunch. It's about the same distance for my family and yours. How about that?"

Liam nodded, relief evident. "That's a great idea."

"All right. You'll tell your father?"

This time it was Liam twitching, but he nodded. "Yeah, I will." He took a deep breath. "Ava and I were going out to dinner tonight, Mom. You want to come with us?"

I stood very still, watching both of them. There was so much hurt on both sides, so much pain. All at once guilt crashed over me at the way I'd been treating my own mother, who only wanted to help me plan the wedding of my dreams. I made a mental promise to try for more patience and less sniping.

Finally, Mrs. Bailey shook her head. "Thank you, that's very nice of you to invite me. But no. I have an early yoga class tomorrow morning, and I need to get back home." She leaned to retrieve her small black purse from a chair and opened it to pull out car keys. Taking a step toward the kitchen door, she paused and turned back to me.

"Ava, I really am very happy for both of you." She offered me a small smile. "I've always thought you're good for him. I'm glad my son's found a woman who makes him so happy. I hope he does the same for you."

I stretched my hand to take Liam's. "He does, every day."

"Good." She nodded. "I'll see you on Sunday."

"I ALMOST FELL OVER when I answered the door and it was her." Liam took a long swig of his beer. "It was like I was sixteen again, and she'd caught me playing hooky. Busted."

"Yeah, well, *you* don't have the memory of yelling about having sex with her son playing on repeat in your mind." I shuddered. "Shoot me now."

We'd finally made it over to our favorite small Italian restaurant, albeit a little later than we'd planned. Our table was tucked into the corner, lit only by a candle in the center. The antipasto platter was half gone, and we'd just ordered our entrees.

Liam shook his head. "She was so worked up by that point, she won't even remember that. Besides, it wasn't you she was mad at. It was me." He snagged a thin strip of prosciutto on his fork. "When she told me about Giff's mom, I felt about this big." He held up his forefinger and thumb about an inch apart. "I knew I should've called her this week. Every morning I thought about it, and then I'd figure out an excuse not to do it. I'm a shitty son."

"Hey." I reached across the table to cover his hand. "No, you're not. It's just . . . . a complicated situation. Your parents haven't exactly made it easy to have a relationship with them. Your mom'll get over it. We'll all talk on Sunday, and everyone will feel better."

"And just what're we going to tell them? All of our parents are pushing for a big wedding. We're like those fish that swim upstream. What are they again?"

I smiled. "Salmon? I don't know. But I think we need to figure out exactly what we want and then present it to all of them as decisions already made. Otherwise, they're going to push us into something we don't want."

"Agreed." Liam pushed the antipasto toward me. "Here, eat that last artichoke heart."

I popped the marinated artichoke into my mouth. "Mmmm, thanks." My lips tilted up as Liam watched me lick the last taste from my fingers. I made sure to slow down and play it up, sucking the tip of my thumb. "So good."

"You're killing me." He closed his eyes. "We need to focus, or we're never going to figure this out. We'll end up spending the weekend in bed and when our parents show up Sunday morning, we'll have to let them do whatever they want."

"Fine." I rolled my eyes. "Take away all my fun."

"Baby, your fun is my fun. Believe me, this isn't easy for me." He finished his beer and set down the bottle. "Okay, so let's start with when. You said Christmas, right?"

"I said I liked the idea of a Christmas wedding. It doesn't have to be then."

Liam pointed one finger at me. "No, this is going to be what we want it to be. If you want a Christmas wedding, that's when we're getting married. Let's choose a date." He pulled out his phone and frowned, scrolling to the calendar. "Friday night or Saturday?"

I considered. "Ideally, I'd like a candlelight ceremony. So maybe Friday night. And let's make it as close to Christmas as possible. Otherwise we run into holiday office parties. Plus, I was thinking I'll already have time off for the holidays, so we could maximize our honeymoon time while minimizing how many vacation days I need to take."

"I love the way you think, maximizing honeymoon time. All right, then it looks like the best date might be . . . . December 21st. What do you think?"

"Winter solstice." I smiled. "The shortest day and the longest night of the year. I like that."

"Me, too." Liam grinned. "So we're in agreement. We're getting married on December 21st."

We sat for a few minutes, looking at each other without speaking, both of us wearing huge silly smiles. Having a definite date made the whole idea so much more real.

"Next we have to figure out where." I took a sip of my wine. "That's going to be a tougher one."

"What're our choices?"

I ticked them off on my fingers. "We could do it here. Father Byers would marry us at Our Lady of Mercy. The downside there is that my mother would have to come down here all the time while we were planning."

Liam cocked his head. "But if we're keeping it small and quiet?"

"You know my mom, right? She'll be making it an event. She won't care if we're getting married at the courthouse and then celebrating at Beans. She'd still expect to trun the show." Our favorite local coffee shop was cute and held sweet memories, but it was barely large enough to hold my family, let alone anyone else.

"Yeah, that's true. Okay, what're our other choices?"

"We could get married closer to where you grew up, closer to your mom and dad."

Liam's lip curled in what was close to a snarl. "Not an option. Move on."

"Oookay. I figured that, but given our next choice, it had to be on the table. We could have our wedding in Seagrove City. Do the ceremony at St. Thomas's, my family's church, where Carl and Ange had theirs."

"All right." Liam nodded. "And what're the pluses and minuses there?"

"Plus is that my mom could handle everything. It'd make her happy. Minuses are that my mom *would* handle everything, and we might lose control. It could spiral."

"Hmmm." Liam fiddled with his empty beer bottle and began to say something else, but he was interrupted by the waiter bringing our food. We were both quiet for a few minutes as we ate. When Liam finally broke the silence, he spoke in measured, considered words.

"I've been thinking about this all week." He wiped off his mouth with the cloth napkin. "The thing is, if at the end of the day, I'm married to you, I don't care how it's done. That's my only goal. And if it makes your mom happy to do a little of the hoopla, that's okay with me, because I love her."

Tears threatened. How in the world did I get so lucky?

There weren't many guys who professed love for their future mothers-in-law. "You just scored major points, you know that, right? And I agree with you. Within reason, of course. I'll agree to some hoopla."

"Got it. Limited hoopla, check. I'll admit, I like the idea of getting married where your brother did. It feels right."

"Me, too. And I'm pretty sure Father Byers would come down and perform the ceremony for us. That'd mean a lot to me, plus it means we could do our pre-Cana here in town and save us trips down the shore."

"Pre-Cana?" Liam's forehead wrinkled.

"Ah, it's the counseling the Church requires before we can get married. I'm not sure how long it is, but it would be easier to do it locally."

"All right. So we've got the ceremony set. What about after? How big a party do we want?"

Apparently my sub-conscious had been grappling with this all week, because the answer to what I wanted popped into my mind and onto my lips. "What about doing a dinner at Cucina Felice? We could have the food ready ahead of time, have my whole family pitch in and we know the menu would be exactly what we want."

Liam grinned. "Well, okay, then. I like that. Do you think your parents will, too?"

"I think so. And it means we have to keep it smaller, because only so many people can fit in the restaurant."

"What about dancing?" He leaned forward a little. "One thing I want, if we're going with any hoopla at all, is to dance with my bride. I want that first dance."

"We could clear enough space for a small dance floor. I want that, too."

"Excellent. Maybe we should go over all the possibilities and nail down what we want to include and what we don't. Then we can lay it out for the parents on Sunday."

"Sounds good." I laid my fork on the side of my plate. "Do

you think we should invite Giff over on Sunday, too? You know he's going to want in on plans. He'd love to be included from the beginning."

"Another great idea. You're full of them. Must be why I'm marrying you."

"Well, it's one reason. Let's start with the engagement party and go right on through the honeymoon. I don't want to leave anything to chance. Or to parents."

"Sure you don't want to start with the honeymoon? I have thoughts on that. Lots of thoughts. Creative thoughts. Ideas for wardrobe, even."

I laughed. "How about this? We save the best for last, and we talk about the honeymoon ideas back at home, where we can . . . expand on the discussion in a more meaningful way."

Liam reached for my hand and brought my hand to his lips. "Baby, I love it when you talk dirty to me. Bring it on."

"I KNOW WHERE I want to go for our honeymoon." Liam pressed his lips to my shoulder. He was lying half over my upper body, still inside me. Our initial discussion about honeymoon destinations had devolved into Liam explaining what he planned to do to me each night after our wedding. Since the result had been three orgasms for me, I was not complaining.

"Oh, really? And where's that?" I brushed my hand over his head, smiling.

"Remember . . ." He kissed a path down from my shoulder, toward my breast. "Remember the night of Julia's birthday party? When I came back to your room, after everyone left."

I shivered. I did remember, though not without a pang of regret for the pain we'd both gone through right after that night. I hadn't been able to trust Liam yet, and I'd intentionally hurt him rather than take a chance on us.

"Yes. I remember."

"I told you that night that your skin was like milk, and you made fun of me. So then I told you it was like the white sand beaches of Anguilla."

I closed my eyes. "That's right. The next day I had to look it up on the map to see where Anguilla is."

"That's where I want to go on our honeymoon. It'll be warm and tropical . . . just the two of us, for a week on the beach. What do you think?"

"Hmm." I pretended to think. "Will you still do that thing to me? What you just did?"

Liam laughed softly. "Every single night, and some mornings, too."

"Then I think I can live with Anguilla and white sand beaches."

He lowered his mouth to draw one pink nipple into his mouth. I hummed in appreciation and then groaned when I felt him growing hard again within me.

"See." He smiled up at me as he shifted to the other breast. "I told you wedding planning can be fun."

Chapter Five

162 Days to W Day

Liam

"BABE, DID YOU GET syrup?" I pulled my head out of the pantry, where I was searching. "I can't find it."

Ava called back from our miniscule dining room, where she was setting the table. "Yeah, it's in the fridge. On the door."

"Thanks." I found the glass bottle and snagged the butter while I was in there, too. I carried both to the table. "Here you go. Anything else?"

"Do you want to put the juice in a pitcher?" Ava folded the last napkin and tucked it on the side of a plate.

I shook my head. "Nah. It'd just mean one more thing to wash after. We can just put the bottle on the table."

"Are you sure?" She caught the edge of her lip between her teeth. "I want to make sure everything looks nice. This is the first time we've had your parents here for a meal. I don't want them to think I'm a hick who doesn't know how to do things right."

"Baby, please. Don't worry about they think." I drew her back against me, sliding my hands over her stomach. "It's all going to be fine." I tried to sound more confident than I felt. I wasn't worried about Ava's table-scape or the food—we made an excellent team in the kitchen—but being in the same room with both my mom and my dad was a potentially volatile situation. Toss in the DiMartinos, and I wasn't sure what to expect.

"Giff should be here in a few minutes. It's good he's coming." Ava twisted her hands together, her classic tell of nerves. "He has a way of making things smoother, you know?"

"Yep. But it's going to be okay anyway. We know what we're going to say. All we need to do is—"

The doorbell rang, and Ava clutched my arms. "My God, they're here."

I kissed the side of her neck. "You go check on the quiche. I'll get the door. It might just be Giff." I said a silent prayer as I walked to the door, though usually, my friend used the back door, and I couldn't remember when he'd ever rung a doorbell here.

"Good morning, Liam!" Mrs. DiMartino pulled my head down to kiss my cheek. "Something smells good in here. Anthony, take that dish into the kitchen, would you—Ava! Where do you want me to put the coffee cake?"

"Ma, I told you not to bring anything." Ava appeared in the archway between the living room and kitchen, a spatula in her hand.

"What? It was nothing. Just an egg casserole and a coffee cake your brother made. I can't come empty-handed, you know that." She kissed her daughter's cheek. "Are we the first ones here?"

"Yeah." I followed my future in-laws into the kitchen. "My mom is on her way. And I guess my dad is, too."

Anthony and Frannie DiMartino exchanged glances. "It'll be fine, son." Mr. DiMartino clapped me on the back. "I'm sure your father only wants you to be happy. He'll be okay. I know it's a tough situation."

I wasn't so sure. I'd called my dad yesterday morning, broken the news of our engagement and invited him to brunch. He'd been uncharacteristically low-key and quiet, offering me congratulations and agreeing that he'd be here for the wedding planning session. But something felt off.

"We're behind you, whatever decisions you make. I know I maybe put a little pressure on you last week . . ." Her mom darted a look in Ava's direction. "But your father and I were talking, and we realized that you two have, uh, challenges that I hadn't been considering. You should have the wedding you want, not the one we think you should have. So." She spread out her hands. "We're fine with whatever you decide. We're behind you."

Over her head, Mr. DiMartino caught my eye and winked.

"Knock-knock, kiddos. Never fear, the wedding planner is here." True to form, Giff sailed through the kitchen door, a dazzling smile on his face. He stopped abruptly and feigned astonishment. "Mrs. D! I swear, you get more beautiful every time I see you. You are *not* old enough to have a daughter get married. Mr. D, you lucky dog, watch out. I just might steal this hot mama away from you."

I rolled my eyes. Any other guy, gay or straight, who talked that way would sound ridiculous. But Giff pulled it off, mostly because it was almost always genuine. He loved people, loved making everyone feel happy and comfortable, and it showed in everything he did. I suspected it was why he was successful in event planning.

"Mama Bailey's just heading to the front door, FYI." He pointed to the front door. "About to make her grand entrance in three . . . two . . . one . . ."

The doorbell rang, right on cue. I shook my head. The man was good.

"Hi, Mom." I opened the door and kissed her cheek. "Thanks for driving down."

"Of course." My mother had clearly recovered from her upset Friday night. She patted my cheek, smiling up at me. "Am I the first one here?"

"No, Ava's parents just got here. And Giff, too." I put my hand to her back, guiding her toward the dining room table.

"Oh, yes, of course, but I meant . . . well." Her mouth tightened.

"No, he's not here. Yet. He said he was coming, though." I raised my voice just a little. "Mr. and Mrs. DiMartino, you remember my mom, Laura."

"So good to see you again, Laura." Mrs. DiMartino stepped forward to enfold her in a hug. "Such good news, isn't it? You must be as excited as we are."

I smiled in gratitude. Ava'd told her parents about my screw-up in neglecting to tell my mom the news, so I knew they'd tread carefully.

"Oh, yes." My mother fussed with the strap of the purse on her shoulder. "I'm very fond of Ava."

"We just love Liam." Ava's mother beamed.

"You've done a fine job raising him. Not easy these days. Believe us, we know." Mr. DiMartino nodded.

My mother's face pinked a bit with pleasure. "Oh, that's right. You have sons, too, don't you?"

"Yes, two of them. And a grandson coming this summer, too."

Mom froze. "Grandchildren. Oh." The faint blush disappeared, leaving her face a pasty white. "I hadn't thought about that. So you're going to be a grandmother . . . soon?" She looked at Ava's mother.

Mrs. DiMartino waved her hand. "Oh, I'm already a Nonna. Our granddaughter Frankie is seven." She squeezed my mother's arm. "It's the best thing in the world, I promise you."

"Well, yes, for you, but I—I'm not ready for that. Not at all." She looked alarmed, and it struck me that it probably had more to do with her younger yoga teacher boyfriend than anything else.

"Mom, come on. The other night you thought Ava was pregnant and you didn't get upset."

"Wait, what?" Mrs. DiMartino whipped her head to look at Ava.

"No, Mom, I'm not pregnant. Calm down, everyone. We were explaining to Liam's mother that we wanted a quiet wedding, and she just thought it might be because . . . but it's not. And I'm not."

"You see, Ava? That's what everyone's going to think if you two sneak off to get married. They're going to assume it's because you had to." Ava's mother looked close to tears. Of course, Antonia. The DiMartinos' oldest daughter had gotten pregnant in high school, crushing long-time dreams and plans for the whole family. When she'd been killed only months after Frankie was born, the grief had been enormous. I remembered anew how important this wedding was to them. To see a daughter safely and happily married . . . it would mean something.

"Mom. Relax." Ava laid a hand on her mother's cheek. "Let's all sit down, okay? Liam and I made pancakes and bacon and quiche. Oh, let's put that egg casserole on a hot pad. Can you grab that, babe?"

Within moments, thanks to my girl's smooth people skills, we were all seated around the table, talking as we passed hot trays of food. My mother had calmed down, and Mrs. DiMartino had pulled herself together, too. Giff was chattering to everyone, putting the whole crowd at ease.

One chair was empty, though. I saw my mother's eyes stray there and then to the door more than once. I surreptitiously glanced at my phone to see if my father had called or left me a message, but there was nothing.

"So . . ." Ava took my hand under the table as she began to speak. "Liam and I've done a lot of talking over the last few days. We realized we needed to decide what we wanted and what was important to us, so that you understood."

"If it's a question of money, you know you don't have to worry." My mother interrupted Ava, and immediately the mood in the room took a downward turn.

"What's that supposed to mean? That we can't pay for our own daughter's wedding?" Mrs. DiMartino's eyes flashed.

"I'm sure that's not what she meant—" Her husband tried to calm her.

"No, but I know you have a big family, and . . . well, we have resources. Liam's father does, I mean."

"We appreciate the offer." Ava's father spoke with finality. "But we are able to give our daughter whatever wedding she likes."

"Fine." Mom threw up her hands. "But did you ever think that they're making decisions based on what they think you can pay? Maybe they want a big wedding, and they don't want to make you feel bad about not being able to afford it."

A shrill whistle cut through the voices. Giff stood up, his fingers at his lips and a frown on his face. "Okay, people, back to your corners. That's enough." When the room was absolutely silent, he shook his head. "Look what you're doing to Ava and Liam. This is a happy time. But if you folks keep it up, they're going to elope to Vegas, and then you'll have to deal with me, because I will be *pissed*." He hissed the last word.

The knock at the door startled everyone. Giff pointed his finger at me. "Stay here. I'll get it. When I get back, I want everyone smiling and getting along."

My mother was the first to speak after Giff stomped from the room. "I apologize. I didn't mean to insinuate—well, anyway. I'm sorry."

"No offense taken." Ava's dad smiled. "We understand, right, Frannie?"

Mrs. DiMartino swallowed. "Of course. We all just want the kids to be happy, right?"

"That's absolutely right." The deep voice in the doorway made my shoulders tense. "It's what we all want." My father bent to kiss Ava's cheek. "I understand felicitations are in order. I'm so happy for you." He looked across at me, and I would've sworn his eyes were misty.

Ava stiffened. She and my father had an uneasy past. The first time they'd met, we'd walked into a room where we didn't know my dad was waiting, and she'd had her legs wrapped around my waist and my hand on her boob. It was an inauspicious beginning, and it didn't get any better. He had, for all intents and purposes, called her a slut and said she was a throwaway girl. He'd referred to her as the kind of girl a guy didn't marry.

Since then, Ava tolerated his presence, but she didn't trust him. And while he put on a smiling front whenever we were all together, I sensed he kept hoping that eventually we'd split.

"Dad." I motioned to the chair across from me. "Why don't you sit down, and I'll get you some coffee?"

"I'll get it." Ava pushed her chair back. When I made a move to protest, she shook her head slightly and bolted for the kitchen.

"Sorry I was late. I was expecting for a few last minute calls, but I think you'll find it was worth the wait." He reached into the slim brown briefcase on his lap. "Liam, I've been making calls since we spoke yesterday, and I've got it all set up." Ava returned with his cup and set it down on the table. "Thank you, my dear." He looked around the table, and I knew he was timing it all for effect. My father was ever the consummate politician.

"How would you two feel about getting married at the National Cathedral in D.C., with your reception at the Mayflower Hotel? I've set it up for early June next year. It's a done deal." He sat back, smiling as though he'd just presented us with the answer to peace in the Middle East.

Ava's eyes were wide as they met mine. I took a deep breath before I spoke. "Dad, we were just telling Mom and Ava's parents that we've decided on everything we want. I appreciate you going to so much trouble, but I wish you hadn't."

Dad leaned back in his chair, arms crossed. "What more could you want? Getting married at the most famous church in our nation's capitol and celebrating at the most exclusive hotel in the city? It's going to be huge. The press coverage—"

"No." Ava ground out the word. "No. Liam doesn't want that, and neither do I."

My father glowered. "With all due respect, Ava, you don't speak for my son. He knows that this type of event is a huge PR opportunity. My son's not going to slink off to get married in some backwater town, even if he is marrying—" He dropped his eyes, but his mouth curled in derision.

"This is *not* a PR opportunity, Dad. It's our wedding, and we're doing it our way. You can shut up and listen, or you can get the hell out. But I'm going to remind you that if you can't show my fiancée the respect she deserves, you won't be included in any of it. We asked you here today because Ava thinks our wedding can be a family affair without people at each other's throats. And by that, of course, I mean you and Mom. But if you can't handle it, there's the door. Use it." I pointed toward the living room.

"Liam, don't be stupid."

"Edward, shut the hell up." My mother stood up, her hands fisted at her sides. "You're going to ruin all of this. You can't help it, I guess. Everything you touch becomes sordid and nasty. You're not going to push our son away. Not from me, anyway." She moved her gaze to Ava. "Ava, why don't you tell us all what you and Liam have decided?"

Ava nodded. "Um, all right. Well, we've set the date." She smiled at me, her first genuine one of the day. "December 21st."

"Of *this* year?" My father's voice was incredulous.

"That's a perfect wedding date. I love it. I can work with that." Giff beamed at us.

"Right before Christmas. Oh, Ava, the church'll be beautiful." Mrs. DiMartino clasped her hands and then backtracked.

"I mean . . . if you decide to get married in the church."

"We are. We thought we'd have Father Byers come up and marry us at St. Thomas's. I called him yesterday, and he's free that day. Well, actually night. We want to have a candlelight ceremony at the church, and then if it's okay with you, we'd like to have the reception at the restaurant."

"Our restaurant?" Ava's father looked as though he might explode with happiness. His eyes were bright, crinkling at the corners as he smiled. "Of course it's okay! More than okay. If that's what you really want, I mean."

"It is." I added my voice. "On two conditions: as long as it won't be too much work for you, and if we can clear space to dance."

"That we can definitely do." Mrs. DiMartino turned to Ava. "We could do a penne in blush sauce, as one of the entrees, and maybe caponata for an appetizer."

"We can talk menu later, Ma." Ava grinned. "But I want to ask Vincent to make the cake."

"He'll be so thrilled. Okay, what else?"

I sat forward and snagged a piece of bacon. "Guest list kept to 70 people. We'll try to have some flexibility about it, but we want to keep it around that number."

"That's going to cut out a lot of the family." Ava's mother frowned.

"Liam, I'll have that many just from our friends." My mother touched my arm. "It's not a realistic number."

"It is, because that's what we want. Most of your friends haven't seen me in years. I wouldn't know them if I fell over them. Close family and close friends only."

My father steepled his fingers and pursed his lips but remained silent. Ava took over where I'd left off. "We want a traditional Catholic service. At the reception, we want food and dancing, but none of the big rituals. We'll cut the cake together, but no bouquet or garter toss. And no DJ. We'll just have music playing." She turned to Giff. "Do you think Jeff would take pictures for us? I know it's a hobby for him, but I love his work."

"I'm sure I can work something out." Giff tapped his bottom lip with one finger. "Is there going to be anything for me to do?"

I laughed. "Most definitely. You're the coordinator. You make it all happen, so Ava and I don't have to worry about anything."

He closed his eyes and made a fist. "Yes! My favorite words in the whole world. 'Make it all happen.' That I can do."

"So you're doing everything with Ava's family?" My mom was unhappy, without a doubt. "What about us? Will there be a rehearsal dinner? Or are your father and I to have no part in this at all?"

"Calm down, Mom. We don't want a rehearsal dinner, or at least nothing formal. Maybe we can just do desserts or something the night before the wedding. But Ava and I talked about it, and if you want to throw us an engagement party—a small one—that's okay."

Mom nodded slowly. "I can do that." With no small difficulty, she glanced at my father. "Edward, would you like to co-host the engagement party with me?"

"This whole thing is ridiculous." My father stood, shoving back his chair. "Do you know how it's going to look, my only son getting married in a Catholic church in some obscure little town? Have you thought about what people will think?"

"I assume they'll think we're having the wedding we wanted, but frankly, Dad, I don't give a damn. And if you cared so much about what people think or about your image, maybe you shouldn't have been screwing two other women when you were married to my mother." I kept it as PG as I could, but anger was growing within me exponentially. I wanted to hit someone . . . preferably my father. Out of deference to Ava's parents, I held back.

"That's it." He threw down his napkin. "Do whatever the hell you want. Fuck up your life. Tie yourself down to this—

this girl. Just don't expect me to stand by smiling like an idiot, pretending I approve."

"Out." I growled through gritted teeth. "Get out of my house, now. I don't ever want to see you again, and if you get any where near Ava or our wedding, I'll make you sorry you did."

There was one silent beat, when I wasn't sure if my father was going to speak again or not. And then he kicked away his chair and stalked out of the dining room. A few seconds later, we heard the door slam so hard the entire wall reverberated with the sound.

I sat down, dropping my head onto hands. A headache pounded in my brain. "I'm sorry about that. I never should've invited him today."

"Liam." My mother's hand touched my arm. "You did the right thing. Both in including him today and in tossing him out. You gave him a chance, and no one can fault you for that."

"Your mother's right." Mr. DiMartino's voice was gruff. "He's your father, no matter what, and you owe him respect. But I'm not going to lie. I'm proud you stood up against him for my daughter just now. That's how a man behaves."

His wife cleared her throat. "Don't you worry about it, sweetie. You did nothing wrong."

Ava slid her hand over my thigh, squeezing. "Thank you, babe. I'm sorry you had to do that."

I covered her fingers with mine, lacing them together. "Always. You know that. You come before anything else."

"Well." Mrs. DiMartino slid her chair back, standing up. "I think we'd better head back home, don't you, Anthony? We left Frankie with Carl and Ange, and we don't want to wear her out so close to her due date. She gets tired so easy now." She picked up her plate. "Ava, let me help you clean up."

"I'll help her." To my shock, my mother stood up, too. She glanced almost shyly between Ava and her mother. "You need to go home. I'll stay and clean up. We can talk about the engagement party."

There was a moment of hesitation, and then Mrs. DiMartino moved to hug my mother. "Thank you for that. Yes, make the plans, and tell me if there's anything you need. Give us the date, and we'll be there."

Ava's parents both hugged us as they left, and then we were alone with my mother, who efficiently cleared the table and rinsed plates. I stayed out of the way, returning to the dining room.

"Beetle, you were magnificent." Giff offered me his fist to bump. "The way you stood up to the Senator . . ." He shook his head. "It made me go all warm and gooey inside."

"Thanks. I wish I hadn't had to do it. I wish he hadn't said that shit."

"Yeah, I know. I get it. But you did good. Now, if you think you're safe with the women in there, I'm heading home to see if Jeff's up yet. We're supposed to drive into the city to have dinner with Amanda tonight."

"Have fun. Tell Jeff we missed him this morning, but I don't blame him for wanting to skip out on the drama. Oh, do me a favor and let Amanda know about the engagement, okay? I don't want her mad at me, too." Amanda was a long-time family friend who Giff and I'd gone to school with. She'd graduated from University of Pennsylvania the same year we'd finished at Birch, and she was nearly done with law school now. We'd never been more than friends, but since her mother was also in politics, we'd been thrown together at events for years. She and Ava'd become buddies, too, over the last few years.

"Will do. Which reminds me. If Mama Bailey's throwing the engagement bash, you need to get an announcement into the papers, pronto. Let me know if you need me to do it. I have contacts."

I groaned. "Really? We have to do that? Are there even newspapers around anymore? I thought everything was on-line now."

"Yes, you have to do it, yes, there are still newspapers . . . and yes, they have on-line components, too. Don't worry your pretty head about it. I'll take care of writing it, and I'll shoot it over to Ava to approve."

I punched his shoulder. "Thanks, pal. I appreciate it."

"Any time. I'll be by this week for us to hammer out the rest of the wedding details."

I wrinkled my brow. "I thought that's what we just did?"

Giff laughed. "Oh, buddy, not hardly. You laid the framework, but we need to figure out attendants, colors, flowers, times, invitations . . . we've only just begun, to quote a sentimental wedding fave."

I sighed. "What happened to our simple, quiet wedding?"

Giff winked at me as he headed for the door. "You'll get it, no worries. But for that to happen, I need to work my magic. Do you trust me?"

"I feel like I'm going to regret saying this, but yes, I do. I think."

"No regrets, my friend." He stepped outside and then paused to look back at me. "Just let it happen."

Chapter Six

129 days to W Day

Ava

"WELL, IF IT ISN'T my own personal stalker."

I glanced up from the menu in front of me and smiled. Julia sauntered to the table and leaned down to hug me as she spoke.

"If you returned phone calls or texts, I wouldn't have to stalk you." I pretended to be mad, but it didn't work. I was too happy to see my friend again.

"Sorry about that. We got back from Hawaii, and it was just insane. Between trying to get the new house in shape, dealing with stuff at work, and Jesse starting his job . . . I've hardly had time to breathe. I kept meaning to call you, but once I'd have time, it'd be almost midnight."

"Doesn't matter. I'm just glad we finally made time to get together." I pointed to the chair across from me, using my left hand. "Sit down so we can order. I'm starved."

"Me, too." Julia was oblivious, apparently, to the ring on my hand. She scanned the menu. "I know I should have the salad, but I really want the burger. And the fries."

I laughed. "Well, wedding boot camp is over, right? So you can afford to indulge a little."

Jules puffed out her cheeks. "I did nothing but indulge for ten days on my honeymoon."

"But did you have a good time?" I leaned forward, my hands folded beneath my chin, left hand slightly forward.

"Oh, I did." She dropped the menu and fell back in her chair. "You have no idea. After all the stress of the wedding, it was like heaven to just lie on the beach, drink as many frou-frou drinks as I wanted . . . oh, and Jesse surprised me with a day at the spa. I had a massage, a mud bath and a facial. And we went snorkeling, and we hiked a little, too. Ave, I didn't want to come home. I'm still scheming how we can move there."

"I bet. So do you notice anything—"

"Good afternoon, ladies. What can I get you to drink?" The waiter stood next to us, smiling.

"Just water for me, please." I bit back a sigh of impatience.

"Same here. Can we order our food now, too? I only have a little while for lunch."

"Sure." He took out his pad and held the pencil poised above it. "What'll you have?"

Julia gave into temptation and ordered the burger and fries. I behaved and asked for a salad, dressing on the side.

"Trying to make me feel bad?" She narrowed her eyes at me.

"No. Remember, I'm not blessed with tall, thin genes. I need to fight the battle of the bulge. Besides, I have a big event coming up, and I want to look good."

"Really? Oh, is that the big party for work? Giff mentioned he was planning something for one of your clients."

"Yeah, he is. But no, I was thinking of something in December."

"That's months away. You have plenty of time, and besides, Ave, you always look good."

I rolled my eyes. "I need to look *especially* good for this event. It's a huge deal. Like, life changing." Giving up on subtlety, I held out my hand, palm down, and waved it around.

Julia's eyes grew round, and her mouth dropped open. "Oh, my God, Ava! Is that . . . it is! Oh my God, when did this happen?" She seized my fingers. "What a beautiful ring. Oh, Ava."

She covered her mouth as tears ran down her cheeks. I fought back my own. No one ever cried alone around me. "Liam proposed the morning after your wedding. It was such a surprise, but Jules, I'm so happy. I can't even tell you."

"Why didn't you call me? Or text me? It's been a month!"

I tugged my hand loose. "Because you were on your honeymoon, and besides, I wanted to tell you in person. That's why I was so persistent this week, wanting to get together. The announcement's going to be in the newspapers this weekend, and Liam's mom is sending out invitations to our engagement party next week."

Julia raised one eyebrow. "Mrs. Bailey's giving you an engagement party?"

I shrugged. "Long story, but yeah. It's going to be at Stefano's down here."

"Not at their house? I'm surprised she agreed to that."

"There's been a lot of compromise going around lately. Liam asked her to have it closer to us so that we can invite our friends. And he didn't want it anywhere near his father, either. Things aren't going well there." I filled her in on the brunch debacle.

"What a jerk." Julia shook her head. "I'm proud of Liam for standing up to him, though. I never thought he had it in him. So you gave up a chance to get married in D.C among the political big shots?"

I shuddered. "Wasn't much of a choice. We know what we want. So it's December 21st, in Seagrove."

Julia clapped her hands. "I can't wait. I'll be there with bells on."

I leaned forward. "I hope you'll be there with a bridesmaid dress on. Will you?"

"Ooooh, I was hoping you were going to ask! Are you having a big wedding party?"

"Nope." I shook my head. "You and Angela as bridesmaids, and Frankie as a flower girl. Liam's having Giff as best man—he swears he can handle both coordinating and best manning—and my brothers as groomsmen. That's it."

"What colors are we wearing?"

"Since there's just the three of you, I figured you could pick out whatever dress you like, and so can Ange. Something Christmasy, you know? Maybe a deep green, or burgundy. We'll talk as it gets closer."

Julia sighed, a dreamy smile on her lips. "Sounds perfect. And what about you? Have you gone dress shopping yet?"

I made a face. "No, but not for lacking of my mother trying. She keeps sending me links to dresses. We're supposed to go after the engagement party. I want something simple. Too much lace and too many ruffles would drown me."

"True. Something classic . . . maybe strapless . . . I mean, if I had boobs like you, I'd totally go strapless."

"Thanks. I think." Our food arrived, and I dug into my salad. "So are you enjoying married life?"

"I really am." Julia's smile turned sappy. "I know we've lived together for a few years, and it shouldn't feel that different, but now that we're official, and moved into our own house, it *feels* different, you know? And every time someone calls me Mrs. Fleming, I want to giggle. I love it."

"I'm glad. I'm happy for you. You and Jesse are a perfect couple."

Julis picked up one of her fries, examining it thoughtfully. "Jesse and I are meant for each other. But we're not perfect. No one is." She raised her eyes to mine. "Jesse told me, after the wedding was over, what happened with my mother. What she said to you. I'm so sorry, Ave. She had no right. You have to believe I don't have a problem with Liam."

I smiled. "I do know, Jules. You've been very understanding about Liam and me, when I know it wasn't easy in the beginning."

"You know, I don't even think about that anymore. Liam's just . . . your boyfriend. Your fiancé, now, I guess. It never even occurs to me to remember that we dated." She reached over the table to squeeze my hand. "It's so clear to anyone who looks that Liam is head over heels in love with you. I can't wait to see you two get married."

"SO JULIA WAS SURPRISED?" Liam held the door for me as we walked into the department store that night.

"Yeah, I'd say so. I had to practically force her head down to see my ring. I guess she's still got that honeymoon glow thing going." I glanced around. "We need to go to customer service, I think."

"How long do you think this is going to take? I'm hungry." Liam's stomach growled, backing up his statement.

"Shouldn't be too long. I mean, how much stuff do we need?" I led him to the desk in the back and smiled at the woman standing there.

"Can I help you?" She was flipping through a pile of receipts.

"I hope so." I leaned on the counter. "We need to open a wedding registry."

The woman's eyes flickered from me to Liam, and her eyes grew appreciative as she checked out my fiancé. I cleared my throat.

"Oh, sure. Just a second." She stapled together a few receipts and dropped them into a drawer. Opening another one, she pulled out a scanning gun. "I'll take your information, and then you use this to register your preferences. Just scan them, and they'll show up on the registry. If any of your guests buy something on the list, it'll be automatically taken off, provided they inform us they're shopping for you."

She took down our names, wedding date, address and phone number, and then she set us loose with the gun. I grinned up at Liam. "Ready?"

It turned out that registering for gifts was a lot more fun than I'd anticipated. We started in the kitchen section. First I found a set of pots and pans that I loved. And then Liam insisted on a new set of knives. We cruised over to the bed and bath area next.

"Oh my gosh, feel these sheets." I held out the package to Liam. "They're like butter."

He rubbed them between his finger and thumb. "Nice. Scan 'em. Make it king-sized, though."

I frowned. "But our bed is a queen."

Liam kissed the top of my head. "It is now, but I'm getting us a new one. A king."

"It won't fit in our bedroom. And why do we need a new bed?"

"Because we do. The one we have now was mine since I started high school. New wife, new bed." He snaked his arms around my middle. "Bigger playground."

I shivered. "I can get behind that, but it still doesn't change the fact that our room is too small for a king-sized bed."

"It might be a little tight for a bit, but when we move, I'm going to make sure we have a big bedroom."

I craned my neck to get a good look at him. "We're moving?"

"Well, eventually." He picked up a hand towel. "I'll never get why people need so many towels of every different size."

"You just do. And don't change the subject. Why do we need to move?"

He moved onto the soap dishes. "Because we're renting right now, and I'd like to buy a house. And I'm assuming we'll need something bigger at some point." Liam cupped my cheek and kissed me, hard. "For when I knock you up."

"Hey." I linked my fingers behind his neck. "You mean when *we* get pregnant." I giggled, knowing how much he hated that phrase.

"Honey, if you get me pregnant, we'll never have to worry about money again. I'll be a medical miracle." He traced the side of my face. "I'm not in a rush for anything. I want us to take our time, enjoy being married for a while. But practicing for making babies is something we can do now. And I want a bigger bed for all that practice."

"I like this plan. I'm a hundred percent behind this plan." I stood on tip-toe to kiss his chin. "Okay, that finished bed and bath. Ready for china and silver?"

Liam made a face. "Why do we need china and silver?"

I shrugged. "I don't know, it's just what you do when you're registering. I guess so we can pass it onto our children. You know, the ones we'll be making in that king-sized bed you're going to buy me."

"But my mother has all that shit, and since I'm an only child, she'll be passing it onto us." He pulled me tighter against him. "So I say we return the scanner doohickey, get takeout, and go home to start practicing."

I snuck my hands down to give his ass a squeeze. "I think that's why I love you. You have the best plans."

He traced the shell of my ear with the tip of his tongue. "Oh, baby. You have no idea."

Chapter Seven

115 days to W Day

Liam

I KNEW IT WAS probably a sign that I was not an enlightened male, but I couldn't help staring at Ava's tits. She was standing in the bathroom, washing her face and brushing her teeth, getting ready for bed. The same thing she did every night. But it never failed to fascinate me.

And tonight, she was wearing a little number she'd picked up earlier this week at her favorite lingerie boutique. It was black, so it set off her creamy skin to perfection. The neckline dipped deep between her breasts so that I got a really good view of them. And damn. I'd been looking at these boobs for over two years. Shit, I'd been groping these boobs for that long. But it never got old. Seeing her like this, getting ready to come to bed with me, made me hard and made me want.

She leaned over the sink to rinse off her face, and the silky little number rode up so I got a good look at her ass, too. I gripped the edge of the bed to keep from reaching out to touch her. Not yet. I knew from experience that making my move while she was still talking was a no-go. Which meant that I should probably be paying attention to what she was saying.

"I'm so glad we let your mom throw the party tonight. It was fun." She reached for a towel to blot her face.

"Yeah, it was." Surprisingly, it was true. My mother had listened to our requests, paid attention to our boundaries, and thrown a lovely dinner that our friends and family all enjoyed. My father had been a significant no-show. Ava worried that I was hurt, but honestly, not having to worry about him was a huge relief. I hadn't heard a word from the Senator since the disaster of the wedding-planning brunch, and my mother claimed she hadn't, either. She'd told me the only communication they had was between their attorneys handling the final details of the divorce settlement.

"What was going on with you and Vincent? I saw you two huddled together for quite a while. I hope he wasn't giving you the big-brother intimidation talk." Ava smoothed cream onto her face.

I laughed. "No, it wasn't that. He was just . . ." I paused. The topic of my talk with Vincent was something I wasn't sure he wanted shared with his little sister.

The party had been going on for about an hour when Ava's brother caught me in a brief moment by myself. He'd grabbed my arm in that steely DiMartino grip and pulled me aside.

"Hey. What's the situation with your friend Amanda?"

I frowned, confused. "What do you mean?"

He jerked his chin in her direction, and I followed his eyes to where she stood, talking to Giff and Jeff. Amanda had cut her hair some time in the last few months, I realized. It hung around her shoulders, and for once, she'd dressed up for tonight. As long as I'd known her, jeans had been her preferred wardrobe, and I remembered battles she'd fought with her mother over dressing up for the political events we'd been required to attend.

But tonight, she was stunning. The red dress she wore clung in the right places, showing off her slender height to its full advantage. And because she was Amanda, she'd dared to wear heels, too, which put her eye-level with Giff.

I turned back to Vincent and repeated, "What do you mean, her deal? She's a friend of mine. We went to high school together. Her mom is on the governor's staff." I shrugged.

Vincent's eyes stayed riveted on her. "Does she live around here? And you never, uh . . . ." He slid his gaze back to me briefly, the question clear.

"No, Vincent. Not that it's any of your . . . well, okay, yeah, I'm marrying your sister, so I guess it *is* your business. But no. Just friends. And yeah, she lives in the city. She's in law school."

Vincent's mouth tightened. "Law school. No shit."

"What's the deal, man?" I put one hand on his shoulder.

"No deal. Just curious. She seeing anyone? Boyfriend?"

I shook my head. "She was dating someone in college, but they broke up a while back. Nothing bad, just going in different directions, far as I know. But Ava might know more. They're pretty good friends. And you know how girls talk."

"Uh, no." Vincent smirked. "This isn't the kind of thing you want to ask your sister about. I'll talk your word for it." He punched me in the arm. "Hey, good party, man. If I don't see you again, thanks. I'll catch you later."

When he'd walked away from me, I was pretty sure he was walking in Amanda's direction. I wasn't positive, but I thought I'd spotted them leaving together a little while later. And I had a feeling they weren't going outside to discuss politics.

"He was just what?" Ava turned off the light in the bathroom and approached the bed. Her boobs jiggled just enough that my mouth went dry.

"Who?" All the blood in my body had rushed in the opposite direction of my brain, and I'd forgotten what we were talking about.

"Vince. What were you talking to him about?" She sounded a little exasperated.

"Oh. You know, just guy stuff."

"Hmmm." Ava stepped closer to me so her knees were nearly touching mine and those luscious tits were right in front of my eyes. "He was staring at Amanda all night. I thought he might be asking you about her."

"Amanda?" I willed my hands to stay by my side and not meander. "Really? I hadn't noticed."

"No?" She parted her legs slightly so that she stood nearly straddling my knees. "So he didn't say anything to you about her?"

"Uh . . ." I swallowed. "Maybe. Yeah, now that you mention it, he might've asked me where she lived. And how I knew her."

"Ah." She came a breath closer and sank down, lining up the heat between her legs with the throbbing between mine. I think my eyes rolled back into my head.

"Baby . . . God, you feel good. And you look . . ." I finally lifted my hands to span her rib cage. "So damned sexy."

"I'm glad you like it." She brushed her lips over mine, the touch as light as a feather. "So why did my brother want to know where Amanda lives?"

I struggled to hold onto enough of my control not to rat out my soon-to-be brother-in-law. "Curiosity?"

Ava laughed softly. She brought her hands up to cup her boobs, lifting them together. "Really?" She circled both thumbs around her nipples until they stood stiff against the material of her nightie.

"Yeah." My mouth dropped opened, and my eyes never left her hands.

"Okay." She began moving against me, sliding her center over my erection. "If you say so."

"I do." I covered her hands with mine, taking on the weight of her breasts.

"Fine." She began to ease away, off my lap.

"Wait a minute. Where're you going?" I grabbed her hips.

Ava laid her hand alongside my cheek. "I'm going to bed. Since you don't want to tell me the whole story . . . I guess this doesn't mean much to you." She swept her other hand down her body.

I pulled her closer. "He didn't tell me anything else, just asked me if Amanda had a boyfriend. And . . ." I took a deep breath. In for a penny, in for a pound. "I think they left the party together."

"Seriously?" She wound her arms around my neck. "Wow. My big brother and Amanda."

"Babe, I don't think either of them left tonight looking for a relationship. At least, nothing long-term. Maybe not any longer than tonight." I palmed her breasts again, this time with my skin directly against the warmth of her body.

"So you think it's just a hook-up?" Ava wriggled a little, fitting herself closer to me.

"Right now, your brother and my friend are the last thing on my mind. The only hook-up I'm interested in is . . . here." I moved one hand to her ass, and with the other, I eased down one side of her nightgown, exposing her breast. Lowering my head, I sucked the taut nipple into my mouth.

"Oh, yes . . ." She writhed, trying to get the part of her that needed me most closer to the hard ridge beneath my zipper.

"I love this." I hooked my finger under the other cup and dragged it down. Now both tits were bared to me, pushed up and just begging for me to enjoy them. Since I was never one to miss an opportunity like that, I didn't hesitate to indulge myself.

"I remember the first time I noticed what a beautiful body you have." I moved my lips against her nipple, and Ava pressed at the back of my head, as though holding me in place. Like I'd ever willingly let go of her.

"Yeah? When was that? That first night in my dorm?"

I shifted to the other side, replaced my mouth with my fingers and pinched that nipple as I licked around the other. When it was hard and wet, I blew softly, smiling when she shivered.

"You won't like it, probably, but it was before . . . before my birthday that year."

To her credit, she didn't even flinch. It made me glad that we'd moved beyond that part of our past. "Mmmhmmm."

I kissed the top of her breast. "I'd come over to meet Julia. She was running late—as usual—but you were there. The door was open, so I went inside to wait. You were asleep on your bed, with one arm over your head and the other to the side. Your shirt had ridden up a little, so I could see the skin on your stomach. I just . . . stood there for I don't know how long, watching you."

Ava wove her fingers through my hair. "Little bit creepy, that." But she kissed me anyway, slanting her open mouth over mine, darting her tongue between my lips until my own tongue wound around hers.

"Maybe." I nipped a kiss at the corner of her mouth. "But it was then that I decided I had to end things with Julia. I couldn't stop thinking about you."

"Sometimes I wish we'd had a different start." Ava lifted up my shirt and pulled it over my head. She tossed it to the floor and then brushed her palms over my chest. "I think about when we have kids, and they ask how we met. But then I realized how we began made us what we are, too. I don't have any regrets."

I dropped back onto the bed, pulling her down with me so that her boobs were crushed into my bare chest. When she lowered her fingers to the button of my pants, I lifted my hips so she could ease off my pants and boxers.

"No regrets." I ground out the words as she took my stiff cock in both her warm hands. "Never. I'd do it all again, and then some. You're worth it all."

She raised herself above me, kneeling, and rubbed the head of my dick against her slick folds. I reared up to take the rosy tip of her breast into my mouth again. I sucked until I had to fall back onto the mattress, and then covered both her tits with my hands, watching her face as she brought herself to climax with my erection, gasping as her back arched.

Just as she hit the peak, she positioned my cock at her entrance and sank down. The spasm of her inner walls pulsed around me as she moved up and down, establishing the rhythm that drove me crazy.

"Liam, I love you." She dropped her lips to my mouth again for one searing kiss before she lifted her head. "What you do to me . . . how you make me feel . . . it's incredible."

"Ava . . . babe . . . I love you. Love you, baby. Oh, God, how you feel. So tight. So fucking good. Not going to make it much—"

And then she cried out, pushing herself down onto me as she moaned my name over and over. It was enough to trigger my own release, and I grasped her hips, bucking madly until the world stopped spinning.

I rolled to my side, holding her against me as I breathed in the scent of her hair. "You know, I thought proposal sex was the best, but I'm thinking now it's got nothing on engagement party sex."

"I'd have to agree." Ava kissed my chest. "Does it always keep getting better, do you think? Or is that just for you and me?"

I grinned as I nuzzled her neck. "I'm not sure it can get any better than this, baby. But I'm more than willing to keep on practicing to find out."

Chapter Eight

87 days to W Day

Ava

"LIAM, I'M LEAVING!" I stood at the bottom of the steps and called up. "See you tonight, okay?"

He leaned over the railing, his hair dripping with water and a towel draped loosely around his hips. "Yeah. Have fun, I'll meet you at the church at six for pre-Cana, right?"

"Right." I blew him a kiss. "Wish me luck."

"You don't need luck. Your only problem is going to be choosing from all the dresses that look perfect on that gorgeous body." He grinned down at me. "Oh, and not being driven nuts by your mother or mine. So . . . yeah, good luck."

I made a face at him and waved. "Thanks so much. Love you."

Giff and my mother had been pestering me to choose a wedding dress for the last three months, but their panic and persistence had ratcheted up another notch within the past three weeks. I couldn't help it that work had kept me busy, or that the few shopping trips I'd made had been less than fruitful. But now they'd made it clear that time had run out. Today was the do or die day, and to that end, they'd pulled out the big guns: my mother, Liam's mother, Angela and Julia were all meeting me at the store. Giff had threatened to come, too, but I'd persuaded him to spend the day with Liam instead.

"You two never hang out, what with your job and his. Go do something fun."

He'd hesitated only briefly. "Maybe you're right. I don't want Beetle thinking I'm paying too much attention to you and forgetting him."

I elbowed him in the ribs. "We've been spending way too much quality time together, Giff. Last night I dreamed we were picking out flowers, and you kept yelling at me. Then you turned into my mother . . ."

"Okay, enough!" Giff clapped his hands over his ears. "I get it. Go and do your girly stuff, but I'll be in constant contact with your mother via text. If you don't finish the day with a dress bought and paid for, I'm going to pick it out myself. Got it, princess?"

I mock-saluted him. "Heard and noted. Go forth and be manly."

Work for both Liam and me had been nearly all-consuming over the past month. He'd finished his graduate degree on schedule in August, though he'd elected not to participate in the December graduation, since the date was too close to the wedding. He was covering classes in the history department for a professor who was on sabbatical. We weren't certain what would happen after that position ended, but we hoped Birch would offer him a full-time professorship of his own.

I'd been handling two challenging new clients, both of whom had almost no experience with social media. Suzanne trusted me to guide them through the process of establishing accounts.

"No one else has your patience, Ava. When they call for

the third time to ask me about their password for 'the Twitter,' I want to scream."

Between our jobs and the wedding plans, my social life was practically non-existent. It'd been almost a month since I'd seen Julia, though we texted often and chatted on the phone at least once a week. I was looking forward to getting some time to catch up with her today.

I was the last to arrive at Martin's Bridal and Formalwear, and everyone else was sitting in the small waiting area. My mother stood up and greeted me with a hug.

"Here she is, the blushing bride." She kissed my cheek and then stood back, examining me with a critical eye. "You've lost weight. Are you eating?"

"Ma, please." I shook my head. "I'm eating, but I'm eating less. And I've been running with Liam. I want to look good for my wedding, right?" I turned to smile at Mrs. Bailey, who offered me her cheek.

"And look here at my nephew!" I leaned over the baby seat, rocking it gently as I touched his tiny nose. "Hello, Joey! Oh, you're getting so big." I glanced up at my sister-in-law. "He's so beautiful, Ange."

"If he'd sleep as much he ate, we'd all be happy." Angela yawned, but she was radiating new-mama happiness. I hugged her tight and thanked her for making the trip up to help me.

Julia sat next to Angela, and I felt a pang of worry when I took a good look at my friend. Her face was pale and pinched, and she had dark circles under her eyes.

"Jules, you okay?" I sank onto the sofa alongside her as my mother went in search of a sales associate to help us. "You look exhausted."

She shook her head and attempted a smile. "Of course, I'm fine. Just working hard. You know how it is." She pointed over my shoulder at the racks of gowns. "So no luck so far?"

I shrugged one shoulder. "I just can't find what I'm looking for, you know? I narrowed it down to three, but all of them have something I don't like. Maybe I'm kidding myself, but shouldn't my wedding gown be exactly what I want?"

"Yep. Absolutely." Julia nodded. "Well, today is the day. We're not leaving until you've chosen it, even if you have to try on every dress in the store."

And for a while, it felt like that was what it was going to take. I stood in the dressing room in just my control-top underwear and my strapless bra, dutifully putting on and taking off gowns. Once the associate had strapped, laced or buttoned me into the new dress, I'd step out onto the small round dais and spin slowly for my audience of critics.

Inevitably, there'd be two who loved it and two who didn't, which meant I had to go back into the stall and start the whole process all over again.

It was nearing lunch time when Julia poked her head into the dressing room. "Hey, can come sit with you for a little bit?"

I patted the bench next to me. "Sure. What's the matter, are they driving you nuts out there?"

She smiled, but it didn't quite reach her eyes. "No, I just wanted a change of scenery. Your mother and Mrs. Bailey are in the racks, looking for new possibilities, and Angela is feeding the baby. I thought I should give her some privacy."

"Oh, that was nice of you. Isn't he the cutest thing? I can't believe he's two months old already. Did I tell you he was almost born in the restaurant?"

Julia shook her head.

"Yeah, it was funny. Well, now it's funny, but at the time it was damn scary. Angela wouldn't stop working, you know, even though my parents and Carl kept threatening to take away her keys to the car. She said she felt better being at the restaurant, so she kept coming in. Liam and I went down there on a Friday night to see about some things at the church for the wedding, and we were all back in the kitchen—all of us but Ange, who was up front working the hostess stand—when this customer comes running back, saying we need to call the ambulance, because some pregnant lady's water just broke all over the floor. We actually sat looking at each other for a few minutes before we figured out it was Angela. We got up front, and she was bent over, having contractions. I guess she'd been having them all day without really knowing. She started screaming how the baby's coming now, and Carl started freaking out that his kid was going to be born in the front of the house."

Julia's eyes were huge. "What happened?"

I waved my hand. "Oh, it was fine. The ambulance came, and they got her to the hospital in time to deliver him. I was so glad it happened when I was actually at home, you know? Liam and I got to hold him right away."

She licked her lips. "Does Liam like babies? I mean . . . are you going to have kids?"

"I hope so. Eventually. Not yet, though. We've talked about it, and we both want to wait until a few years after we get married. We've got time." I elbowed her in the ribs. "You know how it is. You want to be newlyweds for a while. Have fun without having to worry about being responsible all the time."

To my shock, Julia's eyes filled with tears. She dropped her face into her hands and began to sob.

"Jules! What's the matter? What is it?" I wrapped my arm around her shoulder.

She said something, but it was so muffled by her hands and weeping that I couldn't understand her. "What was that?"

Lifting her face, she screwed her eyes shut. "I'm pregnant."

My mouth dropped open in shock. Julia, *pregnant?* I knew she loved kids—or at least she loved Jesse's little brother Desmond—but she'd always said she wanted to wait and have children after her career in journalism was established. She'd been working at an online publication for just a little over a year. I couldn't imagine she'd done this on purpose. Of course, her sobs supported that theory, too.

"We didn't plan it." She wiped at her face. "It happened on our honeymoon, but I just found out about three weeks ago. I had to have tests done, because I was on birth control the whole time."

I found my voice at last. "If you were on birth control, then how on earth did it happen?"

Julia pulled a tissue out of her purse and blew her nose. "Don't you remember the shtick from health class? 'No birth control is a hundred percent effective except abstinence.'" She shook her head. "The doctor said it might've been because my times were screwed up with flying to Hawaii, and I took it too late, or maybe even missed a day. I don't know. She said even if you're very responsible and vigilant, sometimes things just happen." She pulled her loose shirt tight over her stomach, where now I could see a firm bump. "So this just happened."

"Is everything okay though? With the baby?" I couldn't imagine how worried she must be.

Julia nodded. "As far as they can tell. I had to have an amnio and a bunch of blood tests and ultrasounds." She managed a small smile. "It's a girl, in case you wondered."

I swallowed. "Well, that's wonderful, Jules. Congratulations."

Her smile disappeared, and she began to cry again. "No, it's not wonderful. Jesse. . he flipped out. He's not ready, not at all. And between the stress of buying a new house, and his job as a speech pathologist, and now this—" She pointed at her waist. "He's barely talking to me."

Anger washed over me. "That's not fair. I mean, like my mom always says, it takes two to tango. It's not like you went off and did this on your own."

"I know. And he knows. He's not really mad at me, so much as he's just . . . worried."

"Ava?" My mother's voice floated through the louvered doors. "Can I come in a minute?"

"Uh, sure, Ma." I shrugged helplessly at Julia, who began wiping at her face.

The door swung open, and my mother slipped in. I could

see from her expression that she'd overheard. How much, I couldn't be sure.

"Girls, I'm sorry. I'm not an eavesdropper, but I went to knock on the door, and I heard Julia crying." She sat down on the other side of my friend and pulled her into a tight embrace. "Sweetie, it's going to be okay. Don't cry. Don't worry."

A new batch of tears rolled down Julia's cheeks. "But—what're we going to do?"

Ma sighed. "I don't tell this story because I don't want to hurt feelings, but now may be the right time." She glanced at me over Julia's head. "But this doesn't leave the three of us, understand?"

We both nodded, and my mother continued.

"When Anthony and I first got married, he was working at the restaurant all the time. It was his family place, you know, and he wasn't making much. I was going to school nights. I was going to be a lawyer."

A wave of shock hit me. My mother—a lawyer? This was all news to me.

"I wanted to wait and get married after I finished school, but Anthony talked me into marrying him beforehand. He promised he'd support me while I was going to college, and we both said no babies until I'd graduated, passed the bar and had worked for at least two years. We had it all planned out." She smiled, a little sadly.

"We were married all of three months when I started getting sick in the mornings. And then falling asleep on the bus, in the middle of class. I thought I was dying, but of course when I went to the doctor, he told me I was going to have a baby. I was devastated. I felt like my life was over. All my dreams were dead."

"But why?" I felt the need to right the wrongs done to my mother—wrongs that I was just learning about. "Why couldn't you've had the baby and then gone back to school?"

Ma shook her head. "Ava, think about it. Your father was

working crazy hours at the restaurant. He still does, but now he has the boys to help him. Then, it was sometimes twenty-hour days. I'd have had to put the baby into daycare. For one, we couldn't have afforded it, and for two, I wouldn't have it. Once I felt that life inside me, I knew no one could take care of him but me."

"So you quit school." I wanted to cry for my mother, for the dreams that had been lost.

"I did, but Ava, don't you look so sad. Because I'll tell you, the minute I looked at my baby's beautiful face, I knew I'd found a better dream. Carlos was worth more than a hundred law degrees. And so was Vincent, and Antonia, and you." She touched my cheek.

"Julia, you don't have to give up your career. You can keep your job, I'm sure. Things are different now, and your situation is different. But I just want you to remember that things happen for a reason. Babies seldom show up at convenient times." She met my eyes, and I knew we were both thinking of Antonia and little Frankie. "Try not to be upset. And trust your husband. He'll come around. With men it sometimes takes a little longer, because they don't have the life inside them. But he loves you. He'll be fine. You both will." She laid one hand on Julia's stomach. "You all will."

"Ava, I found a dress. I may be completely wrong, but it made me think of you." Mrs. Bailey's face peeked through the door, and her eyebrows shot up at the sight of the three of us. "Oh, I'm sorry. I didn't mean to interrupt."

"Nonsense, you're not. We're just having a little talk." My mother patted Julia's leg and stood up. "Let's see this dress, Laura."

Mrs. Bailey held it back. "Let's let Ava try it on and then we'll all see."

Ma and Liam's mom went out to wait, and the attendant came back in to help me into the gown. She didn't let me look in the mirror the whole time she fastened the buttons and hooks, but I heard Julia's small gasp of pleasure. I crossed all my fingers as I opened the dressing room doors and stepped out onto the small raised platform.

"All right, you can look now."

Ma, Mrs. Bailey and Angela all looked up at me, and for the first time, I saw what I'd been waiting for. The expression on their faces told me the truth: this was the dress.

It was in ivory, since we'd discovered that stark white didn't do a thing for my skin tone. The top of the bodice was all shirred chiffon, a style I'd been avoiding because I was afraid it would make me look too top-heavy. But somehow in this gown, it held my bust in place, accenting without making me look blowsy. It crossed in the front, but with enough fabric that I was decently covered, and then it rose to my shoulders, where it was gathered and accented by tiny seed pearls. There was a band of ruched around my waist, giving me the appearance of an hourglass figure. The skirt flowed seamlessly in layers of weightless chiffon; no ruffles or flounces, just soft cascades that fell to the hemline.

"Oh, Ava." Unshed tears filled my mother's voice. "Oh, you're beautiful."

"Turn around and let us see the back." Angela was all business, but I could hear the underlying emotion.

The back of the gown was simple, with a plunging V to the waistband and a chapel-length train. Small hidden buttons ran down over my backside, but there was no flair or pleating to make my butt look bigger.

"Laura, you found Ava the perfect dress. Thank you." My mother reached over to take Mrs. Bailey's hand and squeeze it.

Liam's mother actually blushed. "I wasn't sure, but it just looked like your style, Ava. The sales lady said it was really for a beach wedding, but I thought, who's going to care what the labels say? If it works, that's all that matters."

I stepped down from the dais carefully and bent to hug my future mother-in-law. "Thank you." I didn't say anything else, but she held me close just a little longer than necessary, giving me what was probably the first genuine embrace we'd ever shared.

"Liam's going to love it." Julia stood to the side dabbing at her eyes. "I can't wait to see his face when he spots you in the church."

"What about a veil?" Angela moved the baby to her shoulder and began whacking at his tiny back for a burp.

I glanced at Ma. "Will Nonna's veil work with this gown?"

"Absolutely." She pressed a hand to her cheek. "It'll be perfect." She turned to the other three women. "Ava's wanted to wear my mother's veil since she was a little girl. It's old-fashioned, but it's simple. It's going to look wonderful." She glanced at me, her face glowing. "My little girl is going to be the most beautiful bride."

"Fabulous. Does that mean we can go have lunch now? I'm famished over here." Angela bent to lay baby Joey back in his car seat. "I'm still eating for two, remember."

"I'm hungry, too." Julia drew in a deep breath and met my eyes. "I'm also eating for two."

There was a second of surprised silence, and then Angela shrieked. "Julia, you're pregnant? Oh, congratulations!"

Jules nodded. "I probably shouldn't have said anything, since I haven't even told my own mother yet, but . . . yeah. I'm due in March." New tears began to leak from her eyes, but this time, I had the feeling they were happy ones. "Jesse and I are having a little girl in March."

There followed the requisite hugs and congratulations, until Ange clapped her hands once. "We can go celebrate this over food. We got a pregnant lady and a breastfeeding lady. Ava, go get out of your perfect dress and let them measure you, or whatever they have to do to make it happen. Ma, grab the tag and go pay the lady." She took Julia's hand. "Julia and I'll go ahead to the restaurant to get us a table." She picked up the car seat handle and tugged Jules behind her.

The woman assisting me had vanished, so I turned to Liam's mom. "Mrs. Bailey, could you help me get out of the dress?"

"Oh, of course." She followed me into the dressing stall and began hunting in the back of the gown for the closures. I watched her in the mirror.

"Isn't that wonderful for Julia and Jesse?" I was being wicked, but I couldn't help myself. "Hmm. Just think, if Liam had stayed with Jules, you might be having your first grandchild next year."

Mrs. Bailey paused, her hands stilled. "Oh. Yes, I guess that's true."

"It was a surprise, though. They didn't plan to start a family so early."

"Hmm." She straightened up and eased the sleeves from my shoulders. "These things can happen." Her fingers closed on my upper arm. "But Ava . . . you're very carefully, aren't you? I mean . . ." She sighed. "I'm thrilled that my son is marrying you. I realize things haven't always been smooth between us, but I know that Liam loves you. And I can see how much you love him. But all the same, I'm just getting used to the idea of being a mother-in-law. I'm not sure I'm quite ready for grandmotherhood yet."

I reached back to cover her hand on my arm. "Yes, we're very careful. Don't worry, Liam and I aren't ready to be parents yet either."

"Good." She smiled at me in the mirror. "Speaking of me not being a grandmother, I wanted to ask you something. Do you think Liam would have a problem with me bringing Alec to the wedding as my date? I don't have to. He understands how it is, but I'd like to have him there. If it's okay with the two of you."

I bit my lip, considering. "I'll talk to Liam, but I think it'll be fine. He knows . . . deep down, Liam knows how much you went through with the Senator. I don't think he wants to hear any details of your dating life." I hastened to add that last part. "But I think he understands." I paused. "Have you . . . heard anything from Liam's dad?"

Mrs. Bailey shook her head as she held the dress for me to step out of it. "Not a word. I left a message for him after the engagement party, telling him it'd gone well, and asking if he wanted to meet to talk about the wedding. I'm trying, Ava. For Liam's sake, I'd like to have at least a show of family unity. But he didn't respond at all. From what I hear through the grapevine, though, things aren't going well for him. There're rumblings that he won't be nominated to run as the incumbent next fall. You know, he'd built his base as a man who supported family values, and with the divorce and all the fallout from the scandal, that's pretty much destroyed."

"I guess I should feel sorry for him, but it's difficult." I pulled my shirt over my head. "Seeing what he did to you and Liam makes it hard to give him any sympathy."

"I don't blame you." Mrs. Bailey nodded. "But for Liam's sake, I wish he'd pull it together and start trying to act like a father. For one day, at least."

"Agreed." I slipped on my shoes and turned around. "I'm all ready. We'd better get over to the restaurant before Jules and Ange eat all the food."

Mrs. Bailey laughed. "All right. And Ava, thank you for including me today. I know you didn't have to do it, but it means something to me."

I smiled. "I'm glad you came. It wouldn't have been the same without you. We're family now."

She smiled. "Family. I like that."

Chapter Nine

60 Days to W Day

Liam

"PROFESSOR BAILEY, COULD I talk to you for a minute?"

I looked up from the tablet where I'd been scanning my notes for the next class. "Uh, sure. Um . . . ?"

"Scarlet. Scarlet Rogers." I recognized her now, vaguely. She was in the lecture I'd just finished, and she always sat in the front row and paid brutally close attention.

"Of course. What can I do for you, Ms. Rogers?"

She giggled, and I had to concentrate on not rolling my eyes. "Um, well, my sorority, the Gamma Eps, is holding its annual Snowflake Gathering in December. We always nominate members of the faculty to attend as our guests, as a way to thank our professors for their hard work and service." She sounded as though she was reciting something she'd memorized, and I was willing to bet she was. "On behalf of Gamma Epsilon, we'd like to invite you to be my guest. Our guest, I mean."

I'd heard rumors about the Snowflake Gathering. It was

listed in campus materials exactly as she'd described it, but the scuttlebutt, which I'd heard when I was here as an undergrad, was that it was a thinly-disguised excuse to include some of the younger professors in a wild party. More than one faculty member—of both sexes—had gotten themselves in trouble there. I was surprised the administration allowed it to go on.

"I'm flattered, Ms. Rogers, but unfortunately, my December is already pretty booked." I flashed her a smile. "I'm getting married."

Her face fell. "You are? Why?"

I laughed. "Well, for a lot of reasons, most of which are not really your business. But the number one reason is that the girl of my dreams said yes." I pulled out my phone and showed Scarlet my background picture. "See? This is my girl. My fiancée."

She gave the picture a cursory glance. "Okay, well . . . thanks anyway." She began to walk away and then turned around. "When is your wedding? The Gathering's at the beginning of the month. Maybe you won't be married by then."

"Thanks, but we'll be busy all December. And even if I wasn't getting married, I still wouldn't be interested." I kept my voice light but firm and hoped she got the message.

"Okay." Her shoulders slumped a little as she opened the door and left. I shook my head, laughing to myself.

"The trials and tribulations of being an attractive young college professor." A familiar voice floated to me from the corner of the room, and I looked up, startled. My father sat at a desk in the far back, watching me.

"Dad." I flattened my hands on the table in front of me. "What're you doing here?"

He didn't move except for one shoulder, which lifted and fell. "I don't really know. I . . . started driving, and I ended up here, on campus. I asked someone if Professor Bailey was teaching today, and he pointed me to this building. I looked into a few classrooms before I found your lecture hall."

"Why? Why now?"

He stood and walked slowly down the rows of chairs toward me, swaying. Tension gripped my neck and shoulders. This was a side to my father I'd never seen, and it scared the shit out of me.

"I fucked up, Liam." There was weariness in his tone, and a self-loathing that put a lump in my own throat. "I fucked up my life. And your mother's, and yours. But you both found a way to go on despite how hard I tried to drag you down with me. And now I'm alone, and I'm ruined, and I'm . . . utterly fucked." He sat down again, this time in the front row, and buried his head in his hands.

"Dad, tell me what's going on." I came around to lean against the table, crossing my arms over my chest.

He shook his head. "The party . . . they've asked me to step down. They said I'm doing more harm than good, and they want to have someone else take my seat. I already knew they weren't going to nominate me for re-election, but I thought they'd at least let me retire with dignity. Ha! Like dignity is something I've earned."

"I'm sorry." It was all I could think to say.

"No, you're not. You don't understand, not really, because you never understood what this means to me. Being Senator . . . it was my dream. Or part of my dream. I'd hoped for . . . well, that doesn't matter now. I've lost that, just like I lost you and your mother."

I closed my eyes and wished Ava were here. She'd know what to do, how to handle this. I just wanted to flee the room, get as far away from my father as I could. But that wasn't an option, because I wasn't a child anymore. I was an adult, a man about to be a husband. Running away wasn't a choice. I had to deal with this.

"Dad, you haven't lost me." I swallowed hard. "And Mom . . . well, yeah, your marriage is over. But I think she still wants us to be a family, in whatever way we can make that happen."

I paused, searching for the next words. "And Ava. You don't really know her, Dad. But she's amazing. I can't believe I get to marry a girl like her. I'm the luckiest guy in the world, because Ava loves me. Because she chose me."

"I tried to destroy that, too." My father sighed.

"Yeah, you did, but we can get past that, if you try." I shoved my hands into my pockets. "All my life, Dad, you've shown me how to take care of what's important. You weren't wrong about how to do that, but you were completely off-base about *what* it is. You taught me that duty, image and appearance should be my top priorities. But really, it's people, and love, and family. If you'd made Mom number one in your life, you would never have cheated on her. If you'd seen me as important, who I really am, not just who you wished I would be, then you would've listened when I said I didn't want to go into politics. And you would've been kinder to Ava."

"It's too late." He was mumbling, and I was having trouble hearing him.

"What? No, it's not too late." I ventured closer and dared to touch his shoulder. "Come home with me, Dad. We'll talk. We can work everything out."

He blinked up at me, a frown creasing his forehead. "It can't be fixed now. Can it?"

I exhaled. "Fixed? I don't know. But you can decide to start over. You can still try for a second chance."

I LEFT MY CAR in the faculty lot and drove my father back to our townhouse in his car. His hands were shaking; I wasn't sure if he'd been drinking or had just had a total mental breakdown, but either way, he didn't need to be behind the wheel. Before we left campus, I sent out a group text to the students of my next session, telling them class was cancelled for the day due to a family emergency. And then I texted Ava.

Dad showed up on campus today. Not sure what's going on, but I'm taking him to our house with me. Just a head's up.

Her reply came a moment later.

Okay, thanks. Are you ok? Need me to come home early?

I smiled. That was my girl, always ready to come to my aid, even when it involved the man who'd insulted her to her face more times than either of us could count.

No, but thanks. Love you, Ave.

Love you too. Good luck. See you tonight.

My father didn't speak as we drove through the streets of Gatbury. He kept his head down, staring at his hands in my lap. I was beginning to worry that whatever was going on might be beyond my ability to help or repair.

Once inside the house, he sat at our tiny kitchen table. I made a pot of coffee and poured him a mug, adding the sugar and milk as I knew he liked it. When I set it before him, he wrapped his hands around it but didn't say anything.

"Dad, tell me what you're thinking." I'd never asked that question before, and frankly it scared the hell out of me.

He finally raised his eyes, and they were stormy and tortured. "I'm thinking that I never gave your mother enough credit for the job she did raising you. It had to be her, because this understanding and compassion didn't come from me."

I smiled ruefully. "I don't know. You always seemed to have compassion. Just not for us."

He nodded. "I made it my motto, you know? 'Put family first.' Then I put mine dead last." He rubbed his forehead. "In the beginning, I was more like you. I told you about my own father, about him teaching me it was expected to have a good political wife and then get your rocks off with someone else. Someone less appropriate. But when I first married your mother, I didn't want that any more than you do now. I thought I'd never need that."

My heart pounded a little faster. "So what changed?"

"I changed. I let myself change. I liked the high it gave me, when pretty women offered themselves to me. I convinced myself it didn't matter, because it was just sex. I told myself your mother wouldn't care." He laughed without humor. "Amazing the things you can convince yourself when you're motivated to do something that feels good."

"But you regret it now?" This was somehow very important to me.

He hesitated. "I regret what it did to my marriage. I regret how it affected you. But I'm not sure that I've changed. I . . . worry that if I had to go back and do it over, I wouldn't change anything, I'd just work harder not to get caught."

I ground my teeth. "That's not going to help you, Dad. You need to see it was wrong. You need to be sorry for what you did, not just sorry you got caught doing it."

"I don't know if I can be that man again, Liam. The man who remembers what's right and what's wrong, not just shades of gray."

"I can help you, if you let me. We can do it. But you need to be honest with me. And there have to be ground rules."

For the next three hours, we talked. I listened to my father pour out the ugliness that had been his life for so long. I didn't give into sympathy; I worked hard to hold him accountable for what he'd done when he tried to make excuses.

By the time Ava came home, he was exhausted, and I'd sent him to our guest room to sleep. I was sitting by myself in the dark kitchen when she came in, carrying bags of takeout from one of our favorite Asian restaurants.

She paused in the doorway for a minute, and then she set down the bags and came to me. Without a word, she wrapped her arms around me and held me tight.

I clung to her, to the solid reality of my girl. "Thank you." My words were muffled against her shirt.

She smoothed her hand over my hair. "For what? Bringing

dinner?"

"No, but that, too. Smells good." I raised my eyes to her face. "For rescuing me from becoming my father. For making it possible for me to be a somewhat decent guy. For saving my life."

She held my face between her hands and leaned down to kiss me. "Baby, don't you know you saved me, too? We were meant to be. Two souls who would've been lost alone."

I linked my hands behind her back. "Promise you'll keep saving me, if I keep saving you?"

She smiled, that slow beautiful curve of her lips that promised me so much more than I'd ever deserve. "Every single day, from now until forever."

Chapter Ten

42 days to W Day

"HOLD IT IN FRONT of you, Ava, so I can get a picture."
Angela held her phone up, frowning as she tried to frame me.
I held the pretty silk teddy—well, what there was of it; it was
pretty skimpy—by both my hands and smiled.

"Oh, look, she's blushing. Isn't that sweet?" One of my
aunts poked another. "The blushing bride."

Behind them, my mother rolled her eyes. "Okay, everyone,
that was the last of the gifts. Julia has the food on the table.
Come help yourselves."

The noise in the room swelled as thirty-plus women rose to
their feet and formed a line. I folded my last bit of lingerie and
replaced it in the box.

"Having a good time, honey?" Ma wrapped her arm around
my shoulder and squeezed.

"I really am." I smiled at her. "Jules outdid herself. Everything is beautiful." I wasn't sure if it was an early nesting phase

or simply the fact that she'd finally accepted and embraced her surprise pregnancy, but Julia had insisted on hosting my shower and then had gone crazy with decorations and food. Aided and abetted as she was by both my mother and Liam's, I was half-afraid the shower was going to out-shine the wedding itself.

"She did an amazing job. Which reminds me, I told her I'd take care of the punch table."

I started to get up. "I guess I should get my food."

My mother pressed by shoulder. "No, sit down. Laura's bringing you a plate. One of the perks of being the bride."

I hid a grin as my mother hurried off. She and Liam's mother weren't exactly best friends yet, but they'd certainly grown closer over the last few months. They'd even gone shopping together for their dresses for the wedding. It made me happy to see them getting along so well.

"Is this seat taken? I brought the bride some jungle juice." Amanda sank onto the love seat next to me, a wicked spark in her eye.

"Ugh, don't say that. I still feel slightly queasy when I think of that night." I stuck out my tongue, trying to suppress the memory of my one and only encounter with high-octane drink that Amanda had shared with me the night we met, at a party Giff and Jeff had thrown. It hadn't ended well for me, unless you call puking into the bushes well.

Amanda laughed. "So are you excited? Countdown's begun, huh?"

I nodded. "The time has really flown. I can't believe we're getting married in six weeks."

"Everything's going okay? No one's freaking out or anything?"

"I don't think so." I sighed. "Not about the wedding anyway."

"Ah." Amanda forked a bit of salad into her mouth. After she swallowed, she glanced at me. "Liam's dad?"

"Yeah. He's been living with us for a few weeks. I understand it. Liam's afraid he's not ready to be on his own. And to give him his due, he's trying. He's seeing a therapist, and he's stepped down from his Senate seat. Liam says he's looking for his own place—he gave up his condo—but . . ." I let my voice trail off.

"But it's not easy to have your future father-in-law living in your guest room, when you're about to be newlyweds." Amanda finished for me.

"Exactly."

"I'm sorry. That's got to be tough on both of you. I hope he moves out soon."

"Here you are, Ava. I hope I got you enough food. Oh, hello, Amanda dear, how are you?"

Amanda stood to kiss Mrs. Bailey's cheek. "I'm good, Mrs. B. And you look great."

"Oh, well . . ." Liam's mother flushed. "Thank you. How are your parents?"

"They're well, thanks. Mom's still working crazy hours, and Dad's on a dig somewhere in the Middle East. But you know, they make it work." She stopped speaking, as though she realized she'd said the wrong thing.

"I'm glad they do." Mrs. Bailey patted her shoulder. "They're lovely people, and I've always considered them good friends. Please give them both my best." She glanced down at me. "Ava, do you need anything? Another drink?"

"No, thanks. I'm good." I watched my future mother-in-law smile and then turn to wend her way through the guests, stopping here and there to speak to those she knew.

"What does Mrs. B think about the Senator taking up residence with you and Liam?" Amanda kept her voice low.

"She didn't like it at first. But now she just doesn't say much. They've run into each other a few times, but they manage to keep it civil. I hope they can hold out during the wedding."

"Me, too." Amanda sipped her punch.

"So, you and my brother? What happened there?" I'd been

waiting for the right opportunity to spring this on her. Now seemed like as good as time as any.

Amanda choked on her drink and began coughing. I pounded her back until she could speak again.

"What do you mean? I don't know what you're talking about." She wiped her mouth with the pretty green shower napkin.

"Cut the crap, Amanda. I know you left our engagement party together. I've been poking at him, but he won't say a word. Just tells me to mind my own."

She picked up her plate and cup. "Then I'm going to take the party line and say the same. Nothing's going on, Ava. I haven't seen Vincent since that night." Her face went red, and my curiosity sparked as she stomped away.

I finished my own food and went in search of a trash can to dump the paper products. I found Julia in the kitchen, opening up cake plates. She was in the full glow of pregnancy now, and she looked adorable in her little maternity dress.

"Jules, thank you so much." I hugged her and dropped a hand to rub her belly. I had full tummy touching privileges, even if no one else did. "How's my little goddaughter doing in there? Cooking up nice?"

Julia laughed. "I don't know about cooking, but she's been kicking like crazy. Jesse swears she's going to be a soccer star. As a matter of fact, he started calling her Mia."

I tilted my head, considering. "Mia Fleming. It has a ring to it, doesn't it? I like it."

"We'll see. I'm not committing to any name yet." She stood back, looking at the cake. "Are you really having a good time, Ave? Are you enjoying your shower?"

"More than you know. It's been perfect. I can't thank you enough."

"Well, you can always return the favor and throw my baby shower. My mom's driving me crazy, wanting to do it. I'd rather have it around here than up there."

"If it can wait until after the wedding, consider it done."

"Speaking of the wedding, how're all the plans coming? Everything running smooth?" Julia rinsed her hands.

I nodded. "As far as I know. Giff sends me weekly updates. He and my mom talk on the phone at least daily, I think."

"That sounds dangerous." She picked up a towel. "And work's going all right?"

"Yeah. Suzanne checks me every day for signs of turning into the Bride from Hell, but so far, she's been disappointed. I make it my mission to stay calm, just to aggravate her."

Julia laughed. "Ava, I'd be more surprised if you did turn into Monster Bride. You always been . . . you know, a rock. The calm one. The girl with the plan. Nothing rattles you." She leaned to kiss my cheek. "You've talked me down more than once, that's for sure." Her hand dropped to her stomach and rubbed the bump.

"Happy to do it." I picked up a plastic fork and snagged an edge of the frosting from the cake. "So Jesse's adjusted to everything? You two doing okay?"

"Better than okay." Jules beamed. "You'd think the whole baby thing was his idea. That he'd totally planned it. He's reading all the books and planning out the nursery. He talks to her every night, and he calls me at least four times a day to check in." She shook her head, but her smile grew bigger.

"And you love every minute of it."

"I really do." She giggled. "I thought this was too early for us. I'm still not sure I'm ready to be a mother, but I know I'm already her mommy. I love her so much, Ave. I can't imagine how much more I can love her when I actually get to hold her."

I swallowed back a lump in my throat. I understood what Julia was saying, but I couldn't quite feel it. And I figured I wouldn't, not until I had my own bump to rub.

Jules caught my expression. "So am I inspiring you? You and Liam thinking about a honeymoon baby, too?"

"Ah, no, I don't think so." I shook my head. "We've talked about kids in pre-Cana classes, and we know we both want them, but we're not ready to nail down when yet. And of course Father Byers says that's okay, because it's not up to us, it's up to God. So I guess we'll have to trust Him, right?"

"How are the classes going? Is Liam doing okay with them?" Julia knew the strict rules of the Church, and she knew Liam had some qualms about what might be expected of him.

"He really is. He's talking about joining the Church, maybe in the next year or so. He says he wants us all to go to Mass as a family when we have kids. Father Byers is just beside himself about that, he's so pleased." I grinned. "The only thing Liam isn't so sure about is that we've decided on a week of abstinence leading up to the wedding. Father Byers manages to ignore the fact that we've been living together most of the time, but he did ask us to consider a sort of fasting when we get to the final week. Liam agreed, but the closer it gets, the less . . . um, enthusiastic he is about it."

"I bet." Julia laughed. "Well, he'll live. And just think how much sweeter it'll make your wedding night." She gave one more glance around the kitchen. "Okay, bride, let's get this cake out there and start serving before I'm tempted to just eat it all myself."

"All right. But Jules, I just wanted to say—thank you, again. And I'm proud of you. I was looking at old pictures the other day, of the two of us in freshman year. God, we were so young. Can you believe where we are now? You're an old married lady, about to be a mama, and I'm going to be a bride, too."

Julia set down the cake and pulled me into a full hug. "I couldn't imagine going through all of it with anyone but my best friend."

I laughed as baby Mia kicked at me. "We've come a long way, baby. And we're not nearly done yet."

Chapter Eleven

28 days to W Day

Liam

"HEY, DAD, ANY NEWS from the real estate agent?" I opened the fridge to find my lunch.

My father was sitting at the kitchen table, a newspaper opened in front of him. "Ah, yes, I'm supposed to see another apartment today, around noon."

"Great." I forced a smile. "Well, I'm out of here. Make sure you lock the door when you go, okay?"

"Will do." He didn't even look up.

I opened the front door and nearly fell over Ava, who was sitting on the cold concrete, her coat wrapped around her against the biting wind. "Whoa! Ava, you okay, babe? What're you doing out here?"

She turned her head and looked up at me, and fear choked me when I saw her eyes filled with tears.

"Babe . . . what is it?" I crouched down and wrapped my arm around her.

She shook her head. "I just needed to talk to you, and I don't ever get any time alone with you anymore. I get up early, and he's there, at the table. I think I'll wait and talk to you after he goes to bed, and he stays up to midnight." She buried her face in her hands. "I started to leave this morning, and he was just sitting there, like a lump, and I couldn't take it anymore. I just sat down here." She shivered, and I held her tighter.

"Come on, baby. Let's get you to my car." I lifted her even as she shook her head.

"I need to go to work. Suzanne'll flip out if I'm late."

"She'll have to flip out, then. Because I'm taking you to Beans, and we're going to sit and talk."

I got Ava settled in the passenger side of the BMW, and then I jogged around to my side, got in and started it up, turning on the heat and the seat warmers. Her teeth were chattering.

As the car heated up, I pulled Ava's phone out of her purse and searched for Suzanne's number. When she picked up, I kept my voice light.

"Hey, Suzanne, it's Liam Bailey. No, I know Ava's not there yet. She's feeling a little under the weather this morning, so I made her stay home. No, nothing serious, I don't think. Just a cold. She's been overdoing it, working so hard." I added that little jab, knowing that Suzanne had been pushing Ava for the last few months. "She might be in this afternoon, but we'll have to see how she feels. I'll let you know. Okay, I'll tell her. Thanks." I hit the end and smiled at Ava.

"She says to tell you to stay home all day and rest. She said you've been looking run down, and she's not surprised you got sick." I shoved the phone back into her handbag and put the car in reverse.

"What about you? Don't you have classes to teach this morning?" She could speak now that she was warming up.

I grinned. "No. I was leaving early just to get out of the house, but I don't have anything until one."

Ava dropped her head onto the back of the seat. "Liam, I

know he's your father. And I understand you're trying to help him out. But God, I just can't take it anymore. He's driving me crazy. I can't be myself in my own house, and I never get any time with you, and I even feel self-conscious having sex. I can't relax. We've got to do something."

"I know. I've been wracking my brain, and I keep asking him about finding an apartment. He says he looks, but each one has something wrong with it. I don't know what to do."

We pulled into the parking lot of Beans So Good, and I held Ava's hand as we went inside. It was relatively empty, since most people had already gotten their coffee fix earlier. We found a table in the back at sat down with our mugs.

"I feel terrible, saying this." Ava traced the handle of her cup. "I feel terrible even feeling it. But I want him out of our house. And I know that puts you in a horrible position. I even thought I could be the one to tell him he needs to move, but each time I think about doing it, I chicken out."

"No, babe, it shouldn't be you. He's my father." I took a sip of my coffee. "I've tried. But each time, he starts thanking me for saving his life. He finally admitted to me the other day that he'd been planning to drive off a bridge the day he came to see me on campus. I guess that came out in his appointment with the therapist. He's on antidepressants now, and he says he's not suicidal anymore. But it's there in the back of my mind. I keep thinking, what if I make him move out and then he does something drastic?"

"We need someone who he can't manipulate. Someone close to the situation, but not involved. We need . . ." Ava raised her eyes to me, and for the first time in weeks, a real smile spread over her face. "I know exactly who we need."

21 days to W Day

Ava

"MRS. BAILEY, I CAN'T thank you enough."

Liam's mother smiled at me as she reached for a napkin from the dispenser in the center of the table. We were eating lunch at the small café down the street from my office.

"I just wish you hadn't waited so long to call me." She wiped off her fingers. "Ava, I've known that man for over thirty years. We may not be married anymore—" She glanced at her watch. "Well, as of about an hour ago, we're not married anymore. But I still know what makes him tick."

"I can't believe how fast it all happened once you got involved."

She laughed. "I know. Amazing how that works."

"Do you think he's really changed? Or was that just part of his manipulating Liam?"

"I hope he's changed. He seemed . . . maybe a little more humble when we talked. But who knows? I think we all need to be mindful of putting ourselves in any position where he can take advantage of us." She shook her head. "Do you know, he actually had the audacity to ask if he could move back in with *me* while he looked for a new place?"

I sighed. "Nothing surprises me anymore."

Mrs. Bailey tilted her head, regarding me. "Are you okay, Ava? You look tired."

"I am. I've been busting my a—my butt at work. And now that the wedding's so close, suddenly there's a million things to do. I thought everything was running smoothly, but Giff and my mother call me all the time. I'm tired of having to decide things. I just want it done. And this is supposed to be a quiet wedding. Can you imagine what it would've been like if we'd done anything bigger?"

"Don't forget that I'm here to help." She patted my hand.

"And try to relax, Ava. You're the center of this whole event. You're the one who's kept everyone going. Don't let it get to you now."

I puffed my cheeks and blew out a breath. "Everyone says that. 'Ava's the calm one. Ava's the rock.' I'm feeling like maybe this rock is about to sink."

10 Days to W Day

Liam

I PICKED UP THE telephone, working hard not to roll my eyes when I saw my dad's name on the screen.

"Hey, Dad, what's up?" I held the phone with my shoulder as I unlocked my car door. My last class had run late, with such lively discussion that everyone stayed well after the session had ended.

The sigh on the other end was grating. "I just needed to talk to you, son. I've had a situation come up here."

Oh, hell to the no. I wasn't going down that road again.

"What's going on?" I kept my voice neutral.

"Lacey called this morning. She had . . . news. It seems, uh . . . it seems that I'm going to be a father. Again."

I sat down in the driver's seat and let my head fall onto the steering wheel. *Fuck.* Why this, why now?

"Are you sure? I mean, you're sure it's yours?" I knew he'd been fucking his secretary off and on, but it wasn't outside the realm of possibility that she might not have been exclusive.

"Yeah, seems like it. We'll do a DNA test, but the timing seems right."

"Well . . . congratulations?" What else could I say? He'd knocked up his secretary. I wondered if there were a greeting card for that situation.

"The thing is, I'm going to try to make it work with Lacey. We're going to get married. Don't worry, I'm keeping it really quiet, but what I was wondering is, will there be room for her at the wedding?"

Shit. I was going to have to dump this on Ava, and I knew my girl was already on the verge of . . . something. I wasn't sure exactly what it was, but for the past few weeks, she'd been slightly closed-off. Tense. She swore everything was fine when I asked, and I figured it was stress over the wedding. The last thing she needed was one more complication.

I cleared my throat. "Sure, Dad. That's fine. I'll let the DiMartinos know." *Oh, that would be a fun conversation, too.* "By the way, when are you planning to get married?"

"Uh, probably this Friday. Just quiet, over at the court-house. You wouldn't want to come and stand up for me, be my witness, would you?"

Sure, nothing better I'd like to do than be my father's best man when he marries the chick he knocked up while he was still married to my mom. No problem.

"Let's see what happens, but maybe."

"I just want to do the right thing this time, you know? I want to give this child the best chance at life. Do all the things right that I screwed up with you. I think this might be the second chance I've been looking for."

*A*va

"HE WHAT?" I HISSED the words.

Liam slumped in his chair. "Knocked up his secretary, decided to marry her, wants to bring her to our wedding. That's the Cliff Notes version."

Something boiled inside me, and I swallowed it down. *Breathe in, breathe out. This isn't Liam's fault.*

It'd been a hell of a day. I was working hard to get everything at the office set up to run while I was away after Christmas, on my honeymoon. And then at four thirty, I'd gotten a call from a distraught client, whose social media accounts had all been shut down just as his biggest push of the current campaign was about to go live. It'd taken me two hours to figure out that he'd posted an image without first securing the rights, and that was why his accounts were suspended. I'd spent another hour calling all my contacts and using every favor owed me to get the suspension revoked. It was now eight-thirty, and I was finally home, where my fiancé was waiting to tell me his dad's good news.

"So can we add her to the guest list? I figured one more person wasn't going to be a big deal."

"And normally it wouldn't, except that everyone's been adding 'just one more person' for the last two weeks. We're pushing a hundred, Liam. That's thirty more than we said."

"A hundred? How did that happen?" He raked his hand through his hair.

"Just like I said. My mom thinks of one person she missed in her first list. Daddy does the same. Your mom, too. We have to invite Angela's parents so they can hold the baby during the ceremony. It all adds up."

"No need to yell at me. It's not my fault." Liam let his head drop back.

"Yeah, well, not mine either." I pushed in my chair. "I'm going upstairs to get a bath."

"Will you call your mom and tell her about Lacey? Or you want me to do it?"

I stopped and answered without turning around. "Oh, no, my friend. That is very much on your shoulders. I already talked to my mother four times today, during a very busy, very stress-filled day. This one's on you." I stamped up the steps and slammed the bedroom door. I ran the bathwater, took off my clothes, climbed into the tub and cried.

7 days to W Day

Liam

THE DAY WAS GRAY and blustery, bitterly cold, and it felt as though snow was not outside the realm of possibility. I hunched my shoulders against the wind as I walked down the sidewalk toward the courthouse. I'd had to park several blocks away, thanks to the influx of holiday shoppers into the city.

It was only four o'clock, but it felt like twilight. The days were growing shorter, the closer we got to the end of the year. Christmas lights shone down from the poles above me, throwing odd shadows as they swaying in the wind. I turned to jog up the steps and into the stone building.

I found my father and Lacey waiting upstairs, just outside the judge's chambers. I vaguely remembered Judge Wallace as a decent man who'd always spoken to me as though I were an adult, even when I was a child. Dad had asked him to perform the ceremony quietly, and he'd agreed.

Lacey stood close to my father, and from the expression on her face, she dreaded seeing me as much as I did her. Her big brown eyes reminded me of a cow's, I thought uncharitably. Her dark blonde hair was done up in an elaborate style. It didn't go at all with the suit she was wearing. She held Dad's hand and regarded me with wariness, which didn't surprise me, considering the last time I'd seen her, she'd been under my father in my mother's bed.

"Liam. Thank you for coming, son." He opened his arms, and I forced myself to return the embrace. He glanced over my shoulder. "Ava's not with you?"

I shook my head. "She couldn't take another day off work, not with the wedding coming up. She's been swamped." And the truth was that I hadn't asked her to come. That just seemed like straw that might break this camel's back. When I'd told her that morning that I was planning to drive up to attend my father's marriage ceremony, an expression I couldn't identify had flickered across her face. But she'd only nodded.

"Senator? Judge Wallace is ready for you now." The judge's admin came out into the hallway and flicked a glance from one of us to the other. We filed into the ante room behind her, and she opened the door to the judge's chambers. She joined us, standing off to one side. I figured she was the second witness, since it didn't appear Lacey had brought anyone.

"Edward." Judge Wallace stood behind his desk. He wore a gray suit and a serious expression.

"Ted." The two men shook hands. "May I introduce my . . . uh, Lacey. And you remember my son Liam?"

"Of course I do. Good to see you again." He extended his hand to me, and I shook it. "You're finished college by now, aren't you? I don't think I've seen you since you graduated. What're you doing now? Following your father's footsteps?"

"No." I might've put a little too much emphasis on the word if the way my father winced was any indication. "No, sir. I'm a history professor down at Birch."

"Ah." He nodded. "Honorable profession. I think I did hear that you're about to be married yourself."

I couldn't help the smile that spread over my face. "Yes, sir. A week from tonight, in fact."

"Well, congratulations to you. I wish you every happiness." Judge Wallace sighed. "Well, let's get underway, shall we?"

It was over in a matter of moments. The words were brief and to the point, without any of the sentiment or meaning I'd heard in other marriage ceremonies. Something Father Byers had said during pre-Cana class flitted through my memory: *These words are ancient, but they stand the test of time. They resonant with us today, because truth and love know no boundary of time or space.*

And then Judge Wallace was shaking my father's hand again, and mine, and offering Lacey congratulations. I signed a form, as did the judge's admin, and we left the chambers.

Standing outside in the hallway again, my dad rubbed his hands together and tried to look happy. "Lacey and I were thinking of catching an early dinner at that little restaurant around the corner. The one that serves the excellent London broil. Would you care to join us?"

Suddenly, I couldn't be here with them for another moment. "No, thanks. I think I'll go home and wait for Ava." I offered him my hand. "Congratulations, Dad. Lacey. I hope you'll be happy."

My father nodded. "Thank you for driving all the way up here, Liam. I appreciate it."

"I know you do." I hesitated for one more time. "I'll see you both next week."

Lacey spoke to me for the first time that afternoon. "Thank you for—letting me come to your wedding. I know it was last minute. But—thanks."

"Sure thing." I thought about what Ava's father said so often. "It's all about family, you know. And now you're part of ours." *For better or for worse,* I thought, but I forced a smile.

Lacey's eyes widened. "Thank you."

I nodded, sketched a wave and turned to go, sprinting down the stairs of the courthouse and out onto the street. I couldn't get home fast enough. All I wanted to see Ava, wrap her in my arms and feel her steadiness around me.

She wasn't there when I opened our front door. I called her name, but it didn't surprise me that she was still at work, with as much extra time as she'd been putting in lately. I opened a bottle of her favorite wine and was just putting together a plate of cheese and crackers when my phone rang. Mrs. DiMartino's name was on the screen.

"Liam, it's me. I hope I'm not interrupting work." That was her typical greeting, and I grinned.

"Not at all. I just got home." I sat down at the kitchen table.

"Well, I might be making a mountain out of a molehill, but I'm worried. You know Ava came down this afternoon."

I frowned. "She did? Why?"

"We talked about it last week. I wanted her to see the table-cloths and linens I'd ordered for the wedding, and she brought down her wedding gown, too, after she picked it up from the store today. Didn't she tell you she was coming?"

Shit. Yes, she had. I remembered it now, vaguely. And this morning, when she'd kissed me good-bye, she'd said she might be late coming back, and if she were too tired, she'd just stay over at her parents' house.

"Yeah, that's right. Sorry, there's been a lot going on. I forgot she was down with you. Everything okay?"

"Well, she got here about an hour ago. She looked at everything I needed to show her, and then she said she needed go out. To be alone. I'm at the restaurant now, but I tried to call her and I didn't get an answer. Like I said, maybe it's nothing, but I'm worried. She didn't look right."

"No, I'm glad you called. She's been under so much stress lately." I stood up and reached for my coat. "Listen, I'm driving down there now. Call me if you hear from her, but I think I know where she might be. Try not to get upset. She's going to be fine."

Ava

I WAS NOT FINE.

I woke up that Friday morning with a sense of dread and doom hanging over me, not at all how I expected to feel a week before my wedding day. But everything at work had been crazy-busy, and I'd been pulling so many extra hours that I practically lived at the office.

Giff kept calling me to remind me of last-minute chores only I could do. I knew I'd hit bottom the day before when I'd snapped at him. "I thought that's why *you* were coordinating the wedding, Giff. So that I don't have to deal with this shit. I don't have time for it."

There was a moment of silence on the other end of the phone. I closed my eyes and swallowed back a sob that surprised me.

"I'm sorry. I didn't mean that. I'm just so fucking tired, and I can't handle one more thing, one more person asking me why something isn't done."

"Peaches, chill. You think you're the first bride who's gone apeshit on me? I've got skin like bronze. Nothing bothers me."

"Still, you're my friend. I love you. I didn't mean to jump on you."

"Ava, let me give you some advice. And you'd better take it. Screw work, screw all the stress. Go get a massage, or a facial, or a pedicure, or whatever floats your boat. You need a break. I'll handle everything from here. You trust me, right?"

I smiled through my tears. "With my very life."

"There you go, that's my peaches. Hang up, grab your coat and get gone. Don't try to explain it to anyone. Just leave. The world will survive without you. Even the world of advertising and social media."

I glanced at the clock. "I *am* supposed to leave a little early this afternoon. I've got to pick up my wedding gown and drive it down to my parents' house. Ma wants it there ahead of time, so I don't have to stuff it in the car with the rest of the stuff next week when I drive down. And she wants me to check out the tablecloths she ordered."

"Excellent. Take off now, go spend some time with Mrs. D, and then take some time for just Ava. And call me tomorrow. I'm willing to bet you'll be a new woman."

After we hung up, I picked up my handbag and my laptop case. I was just shrugging on my coat when Suzanne poked her head into my office.

"Hey, Ava, I just wanted—"

"No." I pointed my finger at my boss. "Just no. I am leaving *now*. I've been working overtime for the past two weeks, killing myself to make sure everything runs smoothly while I'm gone, and I am done. It's not wrong for me to take time off for my honeymoon. I work damn hard all the time, and I deserve a little break. So I'm leaving now, two hours early, and I don't want to hear anything about it."

"Hey." Suzanne held up her hands. "Ava, calm down. I was just coming in to tell you that Mr. Ramp called and was singing your praises. He's thrilled with the campaign, especially your part. And I was going to say, have a good weekend."

I bit my lip and glanced up at Suzanne. "Did it finally happen? Bridezilla? Frankenbride? God, I'm sorry, Suzanne. I'm just . . . overwhelmed, I guess."

She laughed. "I'm not going to say I told you so, because honestly, Ava, you've impressed the hell out of me with all you've been handling. So take your inner Frankenbride and get out of here. I don't want to see your face until Monday."

I didn't even respond. I grabbed my bags and fled.

Chapter Twelve

7 Days to W Day

Liam

IT WAS FULLY DARK by the time I got to the beach. I pulled my car along the curb and climbed out, wrapping my scarf around my face. It was damned cold, and the wind down here by the water only made it worse. Off to the side, across the road, I spotted Ava's small car. I'd had a hunch this was where she'd come. We'd been here once together, about a year ago, and I remembered she'd told me it was where she and Antonia used to go when they wanted to talk away from prying parental ears. It was also where she'd come to cry after her sister died.

I trudged over the small path that led across the dunes and scanned the beach. It was a clear night, and there was enough moonlight that I could make out the waves crashing into the shore. And there, well beyond the reach of the water, huddled on the sand, was my girl.

I fought against the wind to get to her. As I drew closer, I saw she was sitting on a thick blanket of faded green. Her jean-clad legs were drawn up to her body, and she had a knit cap pulled down low over her black hair. Knit gloves covered her hands. At least she'd dressed for the beach in December.

I dropped down next to her. "Hi."

She didn't startle at all or even look my way. "Hi."

"So nice day at the beach, huh?" I pulled my legs in closer to my body heat.

Ava shook her head. "I needed . . . I needed to get away. To think."

Though my heart stuttered, I kept my voice calm. "To think about . . . us?"

She lifted her shoulder, though I could barely tell under all the layers. "No. Us is probably the one thing I'm sure about." She finally looked at me. "But I'm scared shitless about everything else. It's all a mess. We're going to stand up there next week, in front of God and our families and everyone else—a *hundred* people, for the love of blessed Mary—and say things to each other . . . and I'm scared. Everyone thinks I'm the calm one. The girl with the plan, who has everything all together. But what if I'm not? What if I'm just as clueless as everyone else? Then what?"

I wrapped one arm around her shoulders and pulled her to me. "Then you have me. And when you're scared and clueless, I'll be there for you. Just like you are for me. You don't have to be the calm one all the time, Ave. You're allowed to fall apart just like everyone else. I lean on you all the time. Maybe it's time to let go a little and lean on me."

She closed her eyes. "I'm not sure I know how."

"It's easy." I pried one of her gloved hands loose from around her knees. "You just open up your hand and let go, and trust me to catch you." I laced her fingers into my cold ones.

"How can you believe so completely? With everything that's happening . . . your parents . . . how can you be so sure?"

I smiled. "I am sure about us, and I believe in what we are, because when I look at the future, all I see is you and me. And

I know it's all I need."

We were quiet for a few minutes, and I felt her sag against me, the tension finally leaving her body. The wind died down, and everything was still.

"I love you, Liam." She spoke in a whisper that drifted to my ears.

"I love you, Ava." I kissed the small patch of exposed skin on the side of her face. "Next week, we're going to use those ancient words Father Byers talked about when we're in church. But tonight . . . I want to make my own vow to you." I pulled her to stand, holding her hands in both of mine as I gazed down into her eyes.

"Ava Catarine DiMartino, I've loved you for so long that I almost can't remember not loving you. I think my life began the day you finally smiled at me. And I'll spend the rest of my days trying to be the man you see in me. You will always be my first thought when I open my eyes in the morning and my last thought before I close my eyes at night. No matter what life throws at us, I will be by your side. Through the good, the bad, the ugly . . . the difficult and the easy . . . I will never leave you. I don't deserve you, but I'm keeping you anyway. You are my future. You are my love and my life. You are my forever."

Tears were coursing down her cheeks, and her chest rattled with a sob. But she managed to speak anyway.

"Liam Edward Bailey, I didn't want to love you. I tried not to. But letting myself love you was the best decision I've ever made, and I'll keep loving you, growing in love, every day from now until the end of time. You are my best friend, my today, my tomorrow, and no matter what happens, I want to be by your side and get through it together. I don't know what the days to come are going to bring, but as long as it's you and me, together, I know I can deal with them. I don't deserve you, but I'm keeping you anyway. You are my world."

I drew her against me, and we stood there holding each other under the stars while the ocean pounded into the sand.

Chapter Thirteen

December 21st
Wedding Day

Ava

"MA! THERE'S A MAN at the door about the flowers."

Vincent's voice boomed up the steps, and my mother, who was standing behind me with a curling iron in her hand, shook her head. "They're supposed to be delivered to the church, not here. Jesus, Mary and Joseph, can they do nothing right?"

She dropped the curling iron onto my desk. "I'll be right back." She pointed at me in the mirror. "Don't move."

My phone buzzed, and I dared to move just enough to pick it up. It was a text from Liam.

How's it going over there?

I grinned. He was staying with Carl and Angela, getting ready over there with Giff and Jeff.

It's all good here. Two hours til I see you at the altar. Are you ready?

His response was almost immediate.

I've been ready to marry you for three years. I love you, babe.

I love you too. Forever.

"It's all taken care of." My mother, her hair already done, all ready but for the ancient chenille robe she wore, sailed back into my room. "They're taking the flowers to St. Thomas's." She retrieved the curling iron and surveyed me critically. "Almost done here. Oh, my goodness." She pressed her hand to her heart. "Can you believe it's time? You're getting married tonight, Ava." She sniffed and pulled a tissue out of the neckline of her robe. I suspected she had an entire box tucked into her bra for easy reach.

"Ma, don't start again. We just fixed your makeup from before." I fastened her with a stern eye.

"I know, I know. But my baby . . . my baby girl." She took a deep, shuddering breath. "All right. All right. I'm done." She wrapped one more long strand of my hair around the hot iron, held it a moment and then released it. "That's the curls." She picked up an extra-large economy can of hair spray and surrounded me with a cloud that nearly made me lose consciousness. "There. That hair's not moving."

"You use any more hair spray on me, and I won't be moving, either, because I'll be asphyxiated." I waved my hand in front of my face and then examined my hair from all angles. "Just perfect, Ma. Thank you."

"We're here!" Julia called from the hallway. "Are you decent?" She came into the room, the green satin of her dress not even beginning to disguise the large baby bump. She was breathtaking and glowing. Behind her, Angela sighed.

"Your hair and makeup look wonderful. It's almost time to get you in the dress, because Jeff's heading over to take the family pictures in front of the tree." We'd decided to do all the formal family portraits beforehand, and with the house decorated for Christmas, the tree was the perfect backdrop.

My small room was filled to capacity as Ma, Angela and

Julia all helped me with my gown. Frankie was just outside, chattering in excitement. Her hair was in curls that matched mine.

"There. You're all fastened." Ma came around front and clasped her hands together. "You are . . ." She shook her head. "There are no words. You're the most gorgeous bride I've ever seen." She dug for more tissues, and Julia sniffled suspiciously, too.

They helped me with my veil, touched up my lipstick, and I was ready.

Jeff arrived, and we all tramped down the steps for the family pictures, and after those, the bridal party photographs. Angela had opted for a short dress in burgundy, while Frankie wore a sweet gown of white chiffon with red and green accents and a wreath of greenery in her hair. Altogether, we looked like a Christmas card.

"I think this is my favorite part." Giff hugged me carefully. "All the anticipation, all the work . . . it all comes down to this. Family, and love, and all of us together."

"Giff." I held his hand and swallowed back tears. "I don't know what we'd have done without you. Thank you for giving me the exact wedding I wanted."

He shook his head, but I saw the emotion in his eyes. "Peaches, this was a labor of love for two people who mean more to me than . . ." He pressed his lips together. "You and Beetle, you're my family." He took a deep breath. "And enough of the sentiment. Time to make the magic happen."

Once the pictures were finished, Angela, Frankie and Julia left for the church with Carl and Vincent. My parents and I would go separately. We stood in the kitchen as my father fussed with his cufflinks.

"I can't believe this is the last time I'll be in this kitchen as a single girl." I turned in a small circle, taking it all in: the worn linoleum on which I'd learned to dance, the countertops where I'd rolled out hundreds of gnocchi and fettuccine noodles, and the large round tabletop where I'd eaten nearly every meal from birth until eighteen. As I watched, it seemed the shadows of yesterday came forward and flittered around us. I saw my big brothers, tracking mud inside while Ma yelled. Antonia twirling around the table in her cheerleading uniform, her ever-present smile shining bright. My parents holding hands as they sipped coffee while my sister and I did the dishes. I knew that no matter what happened, I'd take these memories with me. They were part of me.

"It's a happy home." Ma slid her hand inside mine. "It has been, hasn't it? So many wonderful things to remember."

"Today's a good day." My father draped his arm around me.

"'And the good days helps us get through the not-so-good days.'" I finished his quotation.

"That's right. See, they do listen, Frannie." He kissed my cheek. "It's all about family, Ava. You're leaving us now, to go out and make your own family, and that's good and right. It's as it should be. But you'll take a piece of us with you, and you'll build your family on that piece."

"Families are messy." My mother spoke slowly. "We're not perfect. We make mistakes. We yell, and we cry, and we say things we don't mean. But at the end of the day, we're still family. We're built on love, and that love doesn't go away. It's with us, part of us, always."

I blinked back sudden tears. "Thank you, both, for this family. I wouldn't be who I am without you or without the family you made." I closed my eyes. "I love you, Ma, Daddy."

We stood in the fading light of the shortest day of the year until the shadows retreated.

THE CHURCH WAS PERFECT. It smelled of evergreen and lit candles. I stood with my father, Angela, Frankie and Julia in the foyer, watching as Carl walked my mother to her seat. Vincent had just seated Mrs. Bailey.

The music changed, and Julia smiled as she started up the aisle. Angela followed close behind, and then Frankie took her turn, walking with uncharacteristic sedateness.

"Our turn." Daddy offered me his arm, and we stepped into the doorway. The congregation had risen to their feet at my mother's cue, and the collective gasp gave me a little thrill.

I couldn't see Liam yet, but Father Byers stood on the altar, beaming at me. I clung to my father's arm as my heart pounded.

A few steps from the end of the aisle, I finally caught sight of my groom. Liam stood tall and unbelievably handsome in his dark suit. When he saw me, his mouth broke into a wide smile, and his eyes gleamed.

We stood at the front of the church while Father Byers intoned the beginning of the service, reminding everyone why we were here, charging us all to speak now if we knew any impediment to this marriage.

And then he was asking my father who presented this woman to be married to this man, and my father was speaking.

"Her mother and I do." He drew me close, kissed my cheek, and passed my hand to Liam. For one breath, he held on to us both, pressing our hands together.

"Be happy."

He stepped back to stand with my mother, and I walked forward with Liam toward the future.

We repeated the timeless words of faith and promise and love that had been handed down to us across the centuries. To have and to hold from this day forward, for better, for worse, for richer, for poorer, in sickness and in health, to love and to cherish til death do us part.

Liam slid a band onto my finger, and I did the same to his. The soloist sang *Ave Maria,* and I presented a small bouquet to the Blessed Mother. Everything else passed in a blur of standing, sitting and kneeling, until Father Byers held our clasped hands.

"Those whom God has joined, let no man put asunder." He smiled at us. "Liam, you may now kiss your bride."

My husband took my hands and held them between his. He leaned his forehead against mine and whispered to me.

"I love you, Ava Catarine Bailey."

His lips covered mine in the most gentle of kisses. It was a brief touch, and yet it contained the promise of a thousand tomorrows together.

THE RESTAURANT WAS DECORATED with Christmas greenery and burgundy bows, with candles on every available surface. We ate and we drank and we danced.

Oh, did we dance.

Liam and I opened the dance floor right after dinner. He held me close as Frank Sinatra crooned about the way I looked tonight.

"Have I told you yet how beautiful you are? How much I love you? How glad I am that you said yes?" Liam's murmur tickled my ear, and I shivered.

"Only about twenty times." I smiled up into his eyes.

"Then I've been remiss. I'll have to make it up to you tonight."

We were spending our wedding night at a hotel near the airport. The next morning, our flight would leave for Anguilla.

"A week on the whitest sand you've ever seen." Liam kissed my nose. "I can't wait."

"I can't, either. But I have to say . . . we had the perfect wedding." Liam turned me, and I caught sight of my parents standing together, my father's arms wrapped around my mom. They watched us, contentment on their faces. Beside them, Carl and Angela sat, the baby in my brother's arms. Vincent leaned against a table, but he wasn't looking at Liam and me. He was talking to Amanda, and she was gazing up at him with an expression in her eyes that I'd never seen there before. Hmmm.

On the other side of the room, Mrs. Bailey stood next to Alec, her boyfriend. He'd turned out to be a decent guy, quiet and kind. Liam and I both liked him. A few tables away, the Senator sat with his new wife, who looked miserably uncomfortable. I hoped for the sake of their child that things would work out for them. I wanted everyone to be happy.

Julia and Jesse were chatting with Giff and Jeff, and I saw Jesse's hand rub his wife's stomach more than once. She covered his hand with hers, and they linked fingers over their unborn child.

Jeff's arm was slung over Giff's shoulder, and when Giff glanced up at him, the love there made my heart glad.

"It really was perfect. Exactly what we wanted." Liam drew my hand to his lips and kissed the back of it as the music faded. Frank Sinatra gave way to Bob Seger singing about old time rock and roll. "And now . . . it's time to party."

LIAM AND I BOTH slept the entire flight to Anguilla. We'd gotten to the airport hotel after two in the morning and caught a few hours of sleep before we had to board the plane.

"I can't believe I'm saying this, but I'm not sure I can stay awake to give you the wedding night you deserve." Liam's voice was muffled on the pillow.

"I know I couldn't stay awake to appreciate it. We'll have our real wedding night tomorrow, when we've slept. Tonight, just hold me." And he did.

It was evening when we arrived at our resort. We were whisked from the front desk to our beachfront villa, which was filled with roses, champagne and chocolates. The attendant left our suitcases in the room and bowed out, smiling at us.

I stood on the lanai, watching the sunset paint the sand a vibrant pink. I felt Liam behind me before I heard his voice.

"There's my beautiful wife." He wrapped his arms beneath mine and held me tight, my back to his front. He bent his head and nuzzled my neck.

"Be careful, sir. I'm a married woman now."

Liam laughed softly. "Come inside and prove it."

I turned in his arms and linked my hands around his neck. "That sounds like a dare."

He shook his head. "It's an invitation." He lowered his lips to mine and kissed me, starting soft and entreating before growing hard and more intense. Desire rose in me, and I pushed aside his shirt as he stripped mine from me.

We fell onto the bed together, a tangle of hands and lips. I only wanted him inside me, and suddenly I couldn't wait.

Liam held himself over me, his erection nudging at my entrance. "I love my wife." He slid into me, and I arched my hips to meet him.

"I love my husband." My words were a gasp of pleasure as need built and I moved faster, urging him to join me. The low ache exploded into a thousand pieces of joy as I cried out his name. Liam tensed moments later, as he found his own release.

I lay in his arms as the room fell into darkness, his heart beat steady against my ear, the assurance of every dream I'd ever dreamed.

WE WOKE EARLY THE next morning and walked on the beach. I stood with my eyes closed, leaning back against my husband as the breeze whispered around us.

"This, right now, this is perfection." Liam rested his cheek against the top of my head. "All the vows I made to you Friday, and the ones I made to you on a much colder beach . . . this is what they mean. This is the beginning of our forever."

I smiled and ran my hands over his arms as they surrounded me, holding me tight. "Our forever. You're mine, and I'm yours. Even when things aren't perfect. Even when they get messy, I still choose you."

"Especially when things get messy." He tilted my head up and covered my lips with his in a kiss that sealed that promise. When he spoke again, it was a whisper against my ear that echoed the ancient words we'd repeated the day before. "I choose you, forever. I choose the good days, the rotten days, the sad days and the happy days. I choose the days of you and me."

THE END

Epilogue

Amanda

"DANCE WITH ME."

I recognized that voice with a thrill of both dread and need. Vincent's hand closed on my shoulder, and I turned slowly.

"Do you think that's a good idea?" I stared at his chest, not willing yet to look him in the eye.

"Why wouldn't it be? What's wrong with two friends dancing at a wedding?"

I shook my head. "But we're not friends, Vincent. We're just . . ." I tried to think of a way to word it. "Two people who slept together. Once."

"I don't remember sleeping that night." He ran his hand down my arm, stopping at my wrist.

I gritted my teeth, forcing myself not to show him what that touch was doing to me. "You know what I mean."

"So we had sex. It was good. Doesn't mean we have to be weird around each other, right? Matter of fact, that's exactly what you said to me, that night."

"I did." I remembered every minute of that night in vivid

color. I wished I didn't.

"So dancing together wouldn't be weird, either. If I hadn't fucked you that night—"

I finally looked up at him. "Seriously? *You* fucked *me?*"

He smiled, his eyes crinkling at the corners. "Keep your voice down if you don't want to make explanations to my parents sitting over there."

I rolled my eyes. I hated complications, and Vincent DiMartino was turning out to be a very big one.

"Anyway, as I was saying, if I hadn't—excuse me, if we hadn't—"

I waved my hand. "Fine, I get what you mean. If that night hadn't happened."

"Right. Then us dancing together at my sister's wedding wouldn't be weird. Some people might think it's weird if we *don't* dance. Two single young people, reasonable attractive . . ."

I raised one eyebrow. "Reasonably attractive? That's not what you said that night."

"Ah, you do remember, huh?" The grin widened. "Okay, counselor, I'll say what I did that night. The sexiest, most beautiful woman I've ever had under me. Is that better?"

It was, and it wasn't. I turned my head to look away, not wanting him to see anything in my eyes.

"Hey." He forced me to look up again, two strong fingers under my chin. "Come on, Amanda. Dance with me. For just one more time, let me put my arms around you. It doesn't have to be anything more than this. Just one dance."

Harry Connick, Jr. was crooning, and the lights were low, and the man in front of me was not only incredibly handsome, he was maybe the best sex I'd ever had. What would it hurt, just one dance?

I let him pull me into his arms, and we moved onto the dance floor. I closed my eyes and hoped I wasn't making a huge mistake.

Yes, Amanda and Vincent will have their own story . . .
JUST ROLL WITH IT will be released in the summer of
2015. Sign up for my newsletter (http://eepurl.com/isWKs) *to*
make sure you know when it's coming.
The best way to thank an author is by leaving a review!
Thanks to my readers who do just that after every book. I
appreciate it more than you know.

Acknowledgements

First and foremost, thanks for this book must go to Leah Fenick. She was the first reader to beg me for more Ava and Liam. I hope you enjoy their happily-ever-after.

My thanks and gratitude to the usual suspects: Stephanie Nelson of Once Upon A Time covers for this gorgeous cover, Stacey Blake of Champagne Formatting for making everything so pretty and making me such lovely teasers, and Amanda Long for her unerring editing skills and advice (and talking me off the ledge more than once).

Appreciation to Mandie Stevens and the PBT team for promotion help, always!

Being an author can be a lonely existence. Even with a full house most days, it is rare that I can talk books, characters, story lines and the every-day neuroses with which writers struggle. I am grateful to my readers who message me just to talk about my books and characters, these people who are so real to us! It's wonderful when you find people who love your imaginary friends as much as you do. By the same token, I'm not sure how many days I'd make it through without Olivia Hardin. Life under the rock rules.

And last but far from least, love and thanks to my awesome family: Clint, Devyn, Greg, Haley, Cate and David, all of whom put up with my snarly moods when I'm deep in the zone, my references to people they don't know, trips to book events and working the tables. I couldn't do it without y'all.

About the Author

Photograph by Heather Batchelder

Tawdra Kandle writes romance, in just about all its forms. She loves unlikely pairings, strong women, sexy guys, hot love scenes and just enough conflict to make it interesting. Her books run from YA paranormal romance (THE KING SERIES), through NA paranormal and contemporary romance (THE SERENDIPITY DUET, PERFECT DISH DUO, THE ONE TRILOGY) to adult contemporary and paramystery romance (CRYSTAL COVE BOOKS and RECIPE FOR DEATH SERIES). She lives in central Florida with a husband, kids, sweet pup and too many cats. And yeah, she rocks purple hair.

You can follow Tawdra here . . .
Facebook (https://www.facebook.com/AuthorTawdraKandle)
Twitter (https://twitter.com/tawdra)
Website (http://tawdrakandle.com)
and of course, sign up for her newsletter (http://eepurl.com/
isWKs)for special tidbits and goodies!

Other books by the author:

Fearless
Breathless
Restless
Endless
The King Series Boxset

Undeniable
Unquenchable

The Posse
The Last One
The First One

Best Served Cold
Just Desserts
I Choose You

Death Fricassee

Stardust on the Sea